The Investigations

by
Frederick T. Mobley

The contents of this work, including, but not limited to, the accuracy of events, people, and places depicted; opinions expressed; permission to use previously published materials included; and any advice given or actions advocated are solely the responsibility of the author, who assumes all liability for said work and indemnifies the publisher against any claims stemming from publication of the work.

All Rights Reserved
Copyright © 2018 by Frederick T. Mobley

No part of this book may be reproduced or transmitted, downloaded, distributed, reverse engineered, or stored in or introduced into any information storage and retrieval system, in any form or by any means, including photocopying and recording, whether electronic or mechanical, now known or hereinafter invented without permission in writing from the publisher.

Dorrance Publishing Co
585 Alpha Drive
Suite 103
Pittsburgh, PA 15238
Visit our website at *www.dorrancebookstore.com*

ISBN: 978-1-4809-4531-9
eISBN: 978-1-4809-4508-1

Characters

Rex Morgan – A successful private detective, well qualified in his chose career.
Anne Towers – Known as "Peggy Lausanne", pretty much free of the Militia's Militia snipers; helps Rex solve his cases.
Captain Hillary – The Berkley Chief of Police, likes to stay informed of events; hates being left out or misinformed.
Eric Wilkson – Appointed Chief of Police, "temporarily".
Sgt. Judy Sturgis – Captain Hillary's secretary.
Wayne Milton – Berkley Police Commissioner.
Milton Bradley – The Director of the FBI after John Covner.
Peter Toberman – The District Attorney.
Cheryl Nickels – An Assistant District Attorney likes to stay on top things.
Larry Flippant – Director of Internal Affairs, carries the nickname, "Headhunter".
Andre' Knowles – Anne Tower's attorney.
Jason Coatis – An officer on the Vice Squad, owner of a nice cottage.
Alex Suemann – Big time Lawyer in the U. S. Justice Department.
Karl Schumacher – Client of Rex and Anne, father of daughter, Frieda.
Frieda Schumacher – Daughter of Karl and Gertrud Schumacher.
Heinrich Hofmann – Owner of Reynolds Warehouse.
Vincent Price – Owner of Edward & Associates.

Fritz –Shady character, friend of Marina, Nicole, and Margaret; person-of-interest

Marina, Nicole, and Margret – Friends of Fritz and Frieda Schumacher, persons-of-interest.

Loui Binoche – Person of Interest in an investigation; a very shady, elusive character.

Ron Belmore – Person of Interest in an investigation.

Heinrich Ottoman – Person of Interest, friend of Karl Schumacher.

Tan Roberts – ABC news reporter; persistent in getting her story coverage.

Harold Jabots – NBC News Live, news reporter.

Samoa's — Rex Morgan's favorite club dinner; a luxurious nightclub.

A NEW REALTOR had come to town and took an interest in the lower income houses on the eastside of town in what was known as the trashed, condemned houses for sale to anyone who would buy them on the condition they'd restore the houses and bring them up to code before moving in. The Oakland Counting Housing Administration had condemned the houses, as far as anyone living in them without bringing them up to safety and housing code of the county. They would have to be inspected and approved during reconstruction.

Rex Morgan, on hearing a real estate was interested in buying and restoring the houses and bringing them up to code, was happy to hear someone had finally decided to make a move and do something. The dilapidated houses were about to be torn down to put something else there, probably a senior housing project or senior apartment complex, but he heard some of those places had been short on staff and neglected, due to NBA. A good part of the money meant for keeping the senior housing and apartments up to par was funneled into other projects that were? were what?

Ha! thought Rex when he heard; more than likely it found its way into someone's pocket or bank account. Rex wondered about this new real estate; he had never heard of Brownstone Realty. "I wonder if some out-of-state realty is trying to make a fast buck or if they're really going to bring those houses up to code?" Rex called Captain Hillary to see if he had heard anything about the realty. "Hey, Captain, how's it going? Nothing going on to make things interesting?" teased Rex.

"I'm glad there's nothing going on; I like it peaceful and quiet, don't you? You gotta have something going on to have excitement?" Hillary shot back.

"Ah nah, I like it quiet and peaceful too. My cases keep me busy and have enough of excitement with them. I don't have a case right now, so I'm catching a breather, but bored. Have you heard of the realtor, Brownstone Realty, interested in those old, dilapidated houses on the what?"

"Yeah, I heard the realty is interested in buying them up, bringing them up to code, and selling them to lower income people. That would be good for two reasons: it would take care of a big, ugly sight and give the low-income families a chance to have a home."

"Do you know anything about the real estate and its owner? I have never heard of that real estate. I wonder if some real estate is figuring on buying the houses and barely fixing them up well enough to pass inspection to make a quick profit," replied Rex.

"You trying to stir something up because you don't have a case right now? Take a breather and relax before you take on another case. Let's hope the realtor's planning to do a good thing with those houses that need a facelift, and you want to shoot it down?" Hillary inquired, a bit annoyed with Rex.

"No, I'm not trying to shoot down anything. Lord knows something needs to be done, but I've never heard of that real estate. Maybe it's just some out-of-state company hoping to make a good profit while trying to make those homes affordable. I hope. Nothing was done to those houses for so long, and now suddenly this company decides to buy them. I wonder if they decided to buy them to fix them up just enough to pass the housing code and sell them to make a profit."

"Being that you don't have a case or anything better to do, check them out, but I hope you're no out, as they say," replied the captain, hoping Rex was wrong.

"I think I'll check them out. If I find anything shady about them, I'll let you know," Rex stated.

"You're a party-pooper, a dream-killer, Rex Morgan! Have a good day. Bye! Hillary slammed the phone down, afraid Rex might be right.

Rex chuckled. Looking up the real estate company on the Internet, Rex found Brownstone Realty was in Harrisburg, Virginia, Harry Salvador the realtor. Checking with the Chamber of Commerce there, they said the realty bought houses and sold them like all real estates, but they didn't have anything on the real estate or the realtor, Harry Salvador.

Rex contacted the county Department of Housing and Urban Development (HUD) to see if they had anything on the Brownstone Realty or its realtor, Harry Salvador. No, they didn't have any violations on the realty or the realtor, but they had come into some questionable code standards with the state and zoning boards and the building department in the courthouse to check on code complaints or violations. Rex drove to Harrisburg, Virginia to the building department of the Harrisburg Courthouse and inquired if there had been any code complaints or violations against Brownstone Realty or its realtor, Harry Salvador.

"You have reasons or concerns for requesting this information, sir?" asked the desk clerk, Nancy Nortel. "Why are you requesting this information, if I might ask?"

"That realty is considering buying trashed houses that have been trashed, and denied to be torn down for years; no realty has made a move to do anything with them until Brownstone took recent interest. These houses are in horrible conditions and it would take a good amount of money to even attempt to restore them. I am wondering why Brownstone is interested in restoring them when they have been condemned for fifteen years."

"You're an investigator, you say?"

"Yes, I am, and I want to know if they are on the level, if there have been any complaints or violations? I am a licensed investigator by the state of California and Berkeley City Hall; I have the right to inquire under the,?" Under the what? replied Rex.

"There had been no violations of code at the time they were remodeled, however, there has been four complaints: two complaints of wire shortening out, and one complaint of a basement wall crack, and with a good rain, there would be moisture on the basement walls creating a smell of mildew; one complaint of sewage seepage in the backyard. In each case, the realty settled without going to court," Nancy Nortel replied.

"Thank you, you have been most helpful."

Rex felt somewhat better, but hated feeling the Brownstone Realty was out to barely meet basic codes without restoring the houses the way they should be. *Captain Hillary will not be happy to hear this*, Rex thought while fixing lunch before calling the captain.

"Well, Captain, I've got the low-down on that Brownstone Realty," stated Rex.

"You're calling to kill my day, aren't you? You have bad news, I can tell!" Captain Hillary replied, exasperated. "Okay, let's hear it."

"I checked with the Harrisburg Virginia Building Department of the City Hall, and there was no code violation when the houses were remodeled, but there have been four complaints. There were two complaints of wire shortening, one complaint of a basement wall cracks, and, with a good rain, moisture on the basement walls creating the smell of mildew, and one complaint of sewage seepage in the backyard. In each case, the realty settled out of court."

"So, they do spotty work, well, you better call the building code department at City Hall and alert. Naturally, they would settle out of court, something that serious. I was hoping the real estate could do some good over there, but now I don't know. You are a thrill to talk to, Rex Morgan!" blurted out the captain, exasperated.

"I was hoping some good would come to town. As far as those houses, they are an ugly sight to the city," replied Rex. "I was hoping for the best, but now I don't know. Some good can still happen if the realty lives up to the codes and does things right. I enjoy making your day," stated Rex, teasingly.

"Yeah, I know you do. Ha-ha! You just made my day, alright. The building code department will have to stay on top of them and see that they do things right, or else face charges, and I will be on them like fleas on a dog!" declared Captain Hillary.

"Yeah, I know you will. I'm just letting you know," replied Rex quietly.

This wouldn't be easy for Brownstone Realty now; they'd have to stand good for restoring those houses if they continued to be interested!

Rex went to the Building Code Department at City Hall and gave them the lowdown on Brownstone Realty from Harrisburg, Virginia, and the complaints. No code violations at the time the houses were remodeled, but afterward, four complaints.

"This will have to be confirmed, so we'll fax the building code department in Harrisburg to confirm what you've said. Thanks for informing us. If what you say is true, we'll be inspecting their work every day or every other day! Maybe twice a day, depending on what we see and if something doesn't add up?" stated the building inspector, Jack Owens.

"You'll inform the Oakland County Housing Administration after you get a fax back?" asked Rex.

"Yes, we'll fax them for confirmation," replied the building inspector.

"I told you only what the Harrisburg City Clerk told me. I drove down there to get that information! You think I made this up? Why would I?"

"I'm not saying you made it up, but we have to confirm it for the record. Thank you for coming forward, we appreciated it."

Rex arrived home, and there was a message on his recorder. "May get hurt stay out of things that don't concern you!" Is the money worth that?"

"Look at my home. When I come home, I relax. I didn't get what I have by taking on big cases. I go out on the patio or deck to grill and enjoy my backyard! I might do that this afternoon."

"I realize you made good by going after those cases, but what price are you willing to pay? As far as you grilling on your deck while you can, enjoy it, but don't rub it in," snarled Hillary.

Rex grinned.

"I see you grinning!" Hillary declared. "Have a nice day and watch yourself. The phone went dead.

"I know," Rex replied, depressed. *Captain Hillary is fun to tease, but he can't handle it. I hear his warning.*

Rex went to the refrigerator to see what there was to cook or to grill out on the deck. There were leftovers from yesterday, a grilled pork chop, black-eyed peas, oaky, coleslaw, and cornbread. For dessert, there was rice pudding, banana pudding, and a mixture of fruits. Rex decided to warm up the leftovers, eat out on the deck, and to relax while watching the squirrels and chipmunks play. Hopefully this would put him in a better mood to consider what Hillary said.

Hillary will have to make do for himself today. I can't handle any more depressing conversations. Since my house is paid for, I should consider handling less risky cases. Being that I have informed the building inspector about the Brownstone Realty, maybe I should let the inspector handle it from here, especially since Brownstone is aware I'm onto their shady practices.

I can't help but wonder how Anne Towers is doing; nobody of late has come to look at her house. She's probably out of the country by now under a different name and disguise. I might not recognize her if I saw her now. I wonder if she thinks about me, or if she's too busy hiding. If she contacted me, it might reveal her location. Hillary's secretary, Sgt. Judy Sturgis, is happy Anne is gone. Ha.

Rex decided to invite Hillary over for a cookout and discuss letting the building inspector handle Brownstone Realty from here. After finishing the left avers, Rex went in the house to call Hillary for a cookout and discuss what they had been talking about. Hillary was delighted to come for a cookout.

"So, you're serious about what we talked about on the phone? I think that is an excellent idea, a lot less risky, and you can still enjoy your home," stated Captain Hillary. "I see Anne's house is still on the market, but nobody has come to look at it?"

"Not of lately. I wonder how she's doing and where she's hiding out," replied Rex.

"You have no idea of where she is?" asked Hillary looking Rex straight in the eye, curious.

"I have no idea where she is. If she contacted me, the firm might be able to trace her. According to Anne, they're that good. She feels it might be years before she can come out of hiding and relax," stated Rex.

"You really don't have any idea where she might be?"

"I would be guessing, a wild guess at best. She's great at concealing her identity. If I saw her on the street, I wouldn't recognize her at all! That's the way she operates. She feels safer that way."

"You think she'll ever show up here, even in disguise?" asked Hillary.

"I seriously doubt it, but if she did, it would be brief, very brief," replied Rex. The questioning went on for five minutes. "Why are you asking? You think she might, or that I'd risk my life for that?" Rex, curious and annoyed, asked, "Why are you pursuing me with these questions?"

"You were really close when she was here, I was curious if you know where she is, that's all," Hillary said, sensing Rex's resentment at being grilled on this subject.

"I don't know where she is; we haven't communicated since she took off. Are you friends of the firm now, or owe them a favor? You have asked a lot of questions about Anne. I don't know where she is, and I haven't talked to her since she left."

"Sorry, I just wondered. I didn't mean any offense, and I'm sorry I pursued it. I don't owe that firm any favor, and I am not friends with them," replied Hillary, offended and wishing he had kept quiet.

"I invited you over for a cookout to let you know I'm going to let the building inspector handle Brownstone Realty, being that I let him know about the realty, but I didn't ask to be grilled about Anne Towers. I don't know where she is and we haven't communicated in any way since she left!" declared Rex.

"I'm sorry about grilling you, I was just curious, that's all," stated Hillary, remorseful. "As far as letting the building inspectors handle the realty from here, that's a good idea, but I am surprised you're dropping this investigation and giving up this easily. You've made Inspector Jack Owens aware of their shady work practices, now let them handle the realty. But I'm still shocked you're giving up an investigation! What changed your mind?"

"I've helped put away the bad guys on too many cases, and some day one of them might decide it's time for payback. I have a nice home and can take less risky cases, even if it means less income," replied Rex. "However, I may stumble into a big case sometime or other, but mainly I will be taking less risky cases now."

"It's a good idea to drop the risky cases and let someone else handle them. You're being smart, having made your nest egg, but I am surprised," stated Hillary, feeling better.

"Well, let's have that cookout and relax," suggested Hillary, heading for the grill. "I like that ideal."

A couple of nights later, shortly after one o'clock, Rex went to bed, being there was nothing else to do. After twenty minutes with the lights out, a knock was at his door. Rex figured it was someone to shut him up or settle a score from a former case. Getting his .357 magnum from beneath a nightstand by his bed, he eased into the living room without turning the lights on and peeked out the blinds to see someone standing at his door. Looking out the peephole, he still didn't recognize who was at his door. Rex stepped to the side of his door.

"Who are you and what do you want?" Rex asked firmly.

"I'm Anne Towers, Rex. Let me in," Anne whispered.

"Sorry, but I don't recognize you," Rex replied, not convinced.

"Of course you don't. I'm in disguise so I wouldn't be recognized. You want me to show my face?"

"How else am I to know it's you? You're really good at disguises," replied Rex.

With that, Anne uncovered her face. Rex quickly opened the door to let her in, and looked up and down the street, but saw no one.

"You sure no one followed you?" Rex asked cautiously.

"Oh, I'm sure. I looked all around me really well," replied Anne. "Aren't you happy to see me, or are you involved with Hillary's secretary?"

"No, I am not involved with Hillary's secretary, and I am happy to see you, but I figured I'd never see you again."

"I had to come back to see you one more time," replied Anne. "I didn't know when I'd see you again, or if I will ever see you again after this."

"Are the hitmen from the firm still after you?" asked Rex concerned.

"I haven't seen any of them for some time now, so I don't know if they're still after me or if they haven't been able to locate me."

"You've been moving around all of this time?" asked Rex.

"For a while, I rented a small house in a small suburb and went to another town to get my mail at a post box."

"How did you do that? The post office must have an established address even to rent a post box," quizzed Rex curious.

"I rented an apartment for four months and then moved, but didn't tell the post office," replied Anne with a smile.

Rex laughed.

Anne spent the night with Rex and decided to stay a week as well, going out in the backyard for cookouts a few times to relax, but never showed her face in front of Rex's house.

"You can stay here as long as you like and feel safe," replied Rex. "I've decided to give up going after big cases involving bad guys and take on only small, less risky cases. I'm financially set to where I don't need those cases anymore. Someone left a message to stop meddling in business that doesn't concern me, and that I could get hurt."

"A wise choice, you won't have to go into hiding like me. I miss my house," stated Anne.

"I can understand, that's is a nice house, but nobody has made any offers lately or moved on it."

"I'm surprised," replied Anne happy at the thought one day she might be able to move back in her house.

Whenever Hillary called, Rex didn't let on Anne was staying with him. Rex was curious as to why Hillary grilled him so much about Anne. What was his reason? Rex wondered about the captain with curiosity. Was he just curious, or was it more than that?

As for the Brownstone Realty, they had put down a big deposit. Their attorneys were working with the Oakland Building Department on the codes and inspections. Rex told Anne about them and how he came across their shady plan before he went to the building inspector. Rex told Anne he decided to let the building inspector handle it from there.

"Wise decision," stated Anne. "Dropping the responsibility in their laps takes the risk off you."

"That's how I feel about it, and Hillary said that was a wise move as well. Hillary came over a few days ago. I invited him over for a cookout and informed him of my decision to back off the risky cases. He grilled me about if I knew where you were. I became annoyed, so he stopped, and now I wonder why he kept pressing me, or if he was just curious."

Anne asked, "He thought you knew where I was and kept grilling you? I don't recognize him as a member or guest of the 'Militia's Militia', but then he might've been a 'sleeper type' member or guest I didn't know about. What happened to Lt. Ottoman who was a deputy?"

"He was arrested and then transported to FBI headquarters for questioning after Hillary was through with him."

"Are you sure? Are you sure he wasn't taken to FBI headquarters and later let go?" Anne asked, scared now.

"Far as I know, he went to FBI headquarters for interrogation," replied Rex. " What happened after he got to FBI headquarters, I don't know."

"One of the big brasses of the FBI might have let him go then," replied Anne concerned. "Well, you can stay here as long as you like and feel safe," stated Rex.

"Thank you, I appreciate that."

While thinking about Captain Hillary, Rex wondered if he and Anne should take an intense undercover look at the captain.

I thought we were over this, but now that Hillary grilled me about Anne, I don't know. Hillary said he was just curious, but to keep questioning me goes a little beyond just being curious, Rex wondered. Rex tried to dismiss it, but the scene kept playing over in his mind. Why?

Rex mentioned this to Anne to hear her thoughts.

"You think Captain Hillary is a 'sleeper' or a sympathizer of the 'Militia's Militia'?" Anne asked, starting to worry.

"I think someone's urged him to question me to see if I knew where you were. I think he's not aware of their motives, so it would be someone he trusts and has confidence in," replied Rex. "It could be from a high office like in the FBI or the Justice Department."

"Here we go again, I was hoping to be through with this. This running is getting old!" declared Anne, becoming depressed.

"I'm sure it is, and I understand, but I wonder why Hillary kept questioning me. He quit when he saw I was annoyed and angry."

"Should I go into hiding again?" asked Anne, hoping not to.

"I don't think you have to right now, but I wonder who put Hillary up to questioning me." replied Rex. "I don't like being grilled like that. I could use your help in finding out."

"Well, okay, here we go again."

"If you're tired of all of this, we can let it ride being I think I persuaded Hillary I didn't know where you were," replied Rex, understanding Anne being tired of this.

"No, if you suspect someone is using Hillary to question you, it's best to find who it is and put a stop to it," stated Anne. "I can go to the police station in disguise to see if I recognize anyone, or pick up any suspicious conversation. Let's do this and put it behind us for good!"

"I'm sorry about this when you come to relax, but Hillary's questioning bugs me," said Rex.

"It would bug me too!"

Anne changed clothes and disguised herself to the point it would be hard, even for Rex, to recognize her in public. Rex dropped Anne off a block from the police station and drove to a parking place on the next block to watch her as she enters the police station.

Anne, looking around, casually saw Hillary in his office on the phone and walked up to the sign-in desk as a sergeant asked her if he could help.

"I'd like to know if I have to get a license for a guard dog in my house," inquired Anne.

"Yes, madam, you do. Do you have one now?"

"No, I'm just asking if I have to."

"Yes, which you can get for twenty dollars over at the license bureau."

"Thank you." Anne walked out the door looking for Rex. She walked a block away as he pulled up.

"Well, I didn't see anyone I recognized, but Hillary was in his office on the phone," stated Anne.

"The only way we're going to find out if he knows any persons-of-interest is to watch where he goes and who he talks to," replied Rex.

Rex and Anne watched where Hillary went for lunch, and followed him to his house, spying from down the street a couple of blocks away, both in disguise.

During the fourth week, a black Lincoln Continental pulled into Hillary's driveway. The man got out, went up to Hillary's door, and knocked on the door. Hillary let him in.

At seeing the guy, Anne became nervous, which Rex noticed.

"You recognize him from the firm?" Rex was perplexed that Hillary had anything to do with a person-of-interest from a shady and criminal subversive organization. Rex wondered if he is a secret "sleeper" or a sympathizer.

"I recognize him as a 'once-in-a-while guest' at the Militia's Militia firm. He'd shake hands with the top brass of the firm and they would go into one of the senior staff's office with the door closed. I didn't dare to snoop or listen should I be seen by someone in my work area. I had my own office, but the senior staff offices were on the other side of the hallway, thirty feet away, and being over there you needed a really good reason," stated Anne.

"Woo, he is a high-ranking member of the Justice Department. He has his own private office and secretary as well!" exclaimed Rex. "That is Alex Spemann. He handles cases in the U.S. Federal District Court and the U.S. Supreme Court! He's no little guy; he's a big wig in the Justice Department! Are you sure about him?" asked Rex, alarmed and nervous, as well as Anne.

"I have seen him. I recognize him. There's no question in my mind about him!" exclaimed Anne.

Rex slowly drove by Hillary's house as Anne wrote down the car license, and then they quickly returned to Rex's house to decide what to do. Both Rex and Anne wondered about Hillary, who was a person-of-interest now.

Where do we go from here? Who do we go to, being that Alex Spemann is such an important person in the Justice Department? If he is with the Militia's Militia, then who else is on the take as well?

"A nice welcome home, huh?" exclaimed Rex, depressed as well as Anne.

"Well, you didn't know about Hillary, but you became suspicious with him continuing to question you. Good thing you found out about him; he pretends to be your friend, but now you don't really know."

"I just wonder if he knows about Alex Spemann, and if Alex put him up to questioning me, or if Hillary is in with him?" replied Rex.

"Good question, but don't be shocked if they both are in it together," stated Anne. "Hillary might have come there when I was at lunch, had a day off, or just a friend keeping his distance."

"I wonder if there might be some bugs planted in my house."

With that, Rex and Anne searched the house from top to bottom, but found nothing.

"Let's have a cookout while we figure what to do about it and relax," suggested Rex.

"Sounds good to me," replied Anne. "Now I wish I had minded my own business, just done my job and went home and not embezzled the firm!" declared Anne, angry with herself. "I had a great salary, vacation time, and benefits."

"A bit late for that now, but you wouldn't have exposed the firm's shady business practices," replied Rex, trying to console Anne.

"True, but I wouldn't have to be in hiding and on the run for my life!" stated Anne.

Rex and Anne went out on the deck for a cookout to relax, and decided what to do about Hillary. After finishing eating, Anne snuggled up to Rex as he wrapped his arms around, and held her. No talking, but they held each other quietly and enjoyed being together again.

A couple days later, Hillary called to check on Rex. "Hey, Rex, we haven't seen or heard from you, and we wondered if you're okay."

"Am I supposed to check in every few days? Nothing has happened here, and I've dropped the Brownstone Realty in the building inspector's lap," declared Rex. "I'm enjoying being at home and taking it easy."

"Judy misses seeing you. She thought you had taken an interest in her and feels let down."

"Are you a matchmaker now?" Rex retorted.

"No, she just thought the two of you had finally hit it off, and I thought so too," replied Hillary. "You still sore about me grilling you about Anne? If you are, I'm sorry."

"Just don't ever do it again. I made it clear I didn't know anything about Anne or where she is, but you kept pressing me! I don't like that, and you know that! I don't know when I'll be coming there if I do come around!" stormed Rex.

"I'm sorry I made you so mad. Is it okay if Judy drops by to visit?" asked Hillary.

"Oh, you're going to use Judy Sturgis to keep tabs on me now?"

"No, I won't do that, but she misses you," replied Hillary, wondering if he had lost Rex, a true friend, for good.

"I've got a bad headache. I've gotta' go," replied Rex, hanging up the phone. Turning to Anne, Rex said, "Hillary might start sending his secretary, Judy Sturgis, to keep tabs on me."

"Great, it sounds like my visit has just ended!" replied Anne, angry Hillary was spoiling everything.

"Maybe after she reports that you haven't been around after a couple of months or so, things will calm down. I need to cool my friendship with Hillary, maybe go on a long vacation."

"There you go, a good move!" replied Anne with a devilish grin. "Or, you could just move!"

"If Hillary is with the firm, a sympathizer, or just being nosey, I'll find a way to break him down to nothing, I swear it!" said Rex in a fit of anger, gritting his teeth.

Anne packed her things and got ready to leave. Anne felt the friendship of Hillary and Rex had ended, especially seeing the anger in his face she had never seen before.

Hillary felt he had lost Rex's friendship, but didn't know what to do. *I should never have pushed him like I did*, Hillary tells himself, *but Alex Spemann wanted me to see if Rex knew where Anne was hiding. Why Alex wanted to know, I don't know, just curious, I guess. Caught in between two friends, with whom do I side? Rex Morgan, a private investigator who has helped solve a lot of cases, versus a bigtime lawyer in the U.S. Justice Department who I grew up and attended the police academy with until we chose our separate careers. Now what do I do being Rex no longer wants to be friends?* Hillary felt strongly Rex no longer trusted him.

Anne had a last cookout with Rex, and they sat together snuggling for what be a last time. Rex knew Anne was packed and ready to disappear like when she showed up. This made Rex angry with Hillary, vowing to strike back at him in some unusual way to bring him down, but in his own time.

Both Anne and Rex called it a night almost at midnight, and Rex eventually fell into a troubled sleep. Waking up the next morning, Rex noticed Anne wasn't in bed next to him and rushed through the house looking for her, but she was gone. Anne slipped out during the night after Rex had fallen asleep. Where she went, Rex had no idea.

"Captain Hillary, you are going to pay for this if you're in the titles MEIN or a sympathizer!" Rex yelled. "But it will be when you least expect it, and in a way you're not expecting! I promise you that!"

Hillary sat in his office and thought about Rex and suddenly, for some reason, felt a cold chill. "This isn't over, as far as Rex is concerned; he will get back at me in some way or another! Darn you, Alex Spemann! You caused me to lose a close friend who might get back at me for grilling him! Darn you, Alex!"

Captain Hillary called Alex Spemann and told him, "You have caused me to lose a close friend, who was a tremendous help in solving cases, by grilling him as to whether or not he knew where Anne was. He firmly stated he didn't, and doesn't, know where Anne is! Now, he is through with me," said Hillary.

"I'm sorry about that. Maybe if you told him I put you up to it, that I'm responsible, he'd get over it," replied Alex.

"I can call him, if he will answer the phone or even talk to me!" replied Hillary, still angry. "Just thinking about him, I had a hard, cold chill, I don't think this is over as far as he is concerned!"

"You think he'll seek revenge? Alex asked, alarmed.

"I don't know, maybe, who knows? But I don't think it's over." "Try calling him and blame me. Keep me informed."

Hillary hung up and called Rex. When the answer machine came on, Hillary left a message. "Rex, this is Captain Hillary, I know you're still angry, but I questioned you because a lawyer in the Justice Department requested it," Hillary stated to an answering machine.

Rex listened, not answering the phone. He continued to follow Hillary from a distance in disguise, which Anne showed him how.

After six weeks of spying on Hillary, Rex was convinced Hillary was totally unaware of Alex Spemann's involvement with the Militia's Militia. Rex invited Hillary to meet him at an open mall, but he requested Hillary not tell anyone. Hillary was confused, but agreed.

"You made me very angry about Anne, but a few nights later she appeared at my door after I had already gone to bed. She's good at that, believe me! I don't know where she came from, and I didn't ask, but I told her about you grilling me and we decided to spy on you. We saw Alex Spemann pull in your driveway and enter your house. Anne recognized him immediately as a once-in-a-while guest at the firm she worked for, and he shook hands with the top staff and went in one of their offices. Anne says Alex Spemann is a Militia's Militia sympathizer or 'sleeper'. She became nervous seeing him at your door! She wonders about you, but I wonder if you know about him. Anne is gone now; she waited until I was sleeping, and then just up and disappeared which she is good at, really good!"

Hillary was in total shock at hearing this. "You have to be kidding. Alex Spemann a sympathizer of the Militia's Militia? I can't believe that! I've known him for years; we grew up together and were in the police academy! Where is Anne now? I need to question her about this. I can't simply go by hearsay!"

"I have no idea where Anne is now. You asked if I mind if Judy Sturgis comes over? We figured you were going to have Judy keep tabs on me, so Anne left during the night after we had gone to bed!" exclaimed Rex. "Anne could be anywhere by now, and she didn't tell me where she's going so you wouldn't be able to get her through me! I can't blame her for that!"

"How am I supposed to know if what she said is true or not? I can't believe Alex Spemann is involved with the Militia's Militia. That blows my mind! It would have to go through the Justice Department to deal with him, if he is involved!"

"Well, he's involved, Anne got really nervous on seeing him, I mean really nervous!" exclaimed Rex. "Anne is highly suspicious of you as well now. She wonders if you're a 'sleeper type', a sympathizer, or an occasional guest, but I told her I didn't think you were as far as I know."

"You don't think I'm involved, but you don't know?" asked Hillary, astounded. "For as long as we have been friends, you don't know me better than that? I'm hurt!"

"Alex Spemann, who Anne recognized immediately, was seen pulling in your driveway and entering your house! He didn't break in, you let him in!" declared Rex.

"He's a friend I grew up with, and we were in the police academy together, as I've told you! You have only her word, and maybe Alex was there on official business, if he was there!"

"He was there every once-in-a-while, and if he was on official business, I don't think Anne would've been so nervous. I doubt they would have been shaking hands in a friendly manner," replied Rex.

"Did she hear what they talked about?" quizzed Hillary. "As far as them shaking hands, they might be helping him or had him checking on someone they suspected!"

"She only saw him there. If she had gone snooping around, she would've been in big trouble! Anne's office is far across the hall from the staffs' offices; it would've been obvious why she was there," replied Rex.

"She has no idea why he was there then, does she?" stated Hillary annoyed that Rex accused Alex of being involved with the Militia's Militia.

"True, but he still looks guilty!" snarled Rex. "Are you excusing him, Captain?"

"You've heard 'innocent until proven guilty', right? Prove it before you start accusing people! Statements without proof is slandering a U.S. government official, which is a federal offense!"

"Well, belonging to a subversive organization is an illegal offense, especially for a government official, and you know it as well! If Anne contacts me, I'll relay your message," replied Rex.

"From what she's gone through, and the militia may still be after her, I can imagine," replied Hillary. "But she needs to prove Alex was involved with the militia. I am not involved in any way or form with them! I thought you knew me better than that!"

"Okay, but you grilling me about Anne made you look suspicious, and Anne and I still wonder!"

Rex returned home to wait for Anne to contact him and to relay what Hillary said.

Four months later, Rex received an invitation for a free meal of the month. Rex, not familiar with the place, looked it up in the phone directory; a small café on the outskirts of town. Rex wondered what prompted this, but had a hunch why and grinned.

Arriving at the eatery, dressed casual, Rex sat at a table in the back corner, so he could watch who entered and left. A bag lady with a limp slowly came to his table and asked if Rex would buy her a cup of coffee as the waiter came to show her the door.

"That's okay, she wants a cup of coffee and I could use one too," Rex told the waiter. After the waiter left for the coffee, Rex laughed. "You sure look the part, madam."

"Good, that's what I intended." Anne grinned. "Have you found anything on Hillary and Alex Spemann?"

Rex started to tell Anne what Hillary said, but waited as the waiter sat their coffees down.

"Would you like something to order?" asked the waiter.

Rex and Anne looked over the menus. Rex ordered the meatloaf and salad, and Anne ordered a turkey sandwich platter.

"Well, that should take a bit to cook," Rex said as the waiter put in the two orders. Rex told Anne what Hillary told him. "Hillary wants proof Alex is involved."

"It's possible Hillary is telling the truth, but I wouldn't take it at face value; don't accept it without checking it out first. Hillary might turn out to be secretly involved," Anne cautioned.

"You just don't trust Hillary, do you?" Rex asked.

"No, not after seeing Spemann at Hillary's door and entering his house. Doesn't that bother you?"

"No, after what you've gone through, I can understand, but Hillary and I have worked together for some years now. It's hard for me to even think of Hillary as a 'sleeper' much less a member or guest," replied Rex.

"I know, and I hate the thought of breaking you two up, but what if he is involved?" Anne whispered.

"If he is, I'd drop his friendship like dead weight, but I don't feel he is. He was shocked at the idea of Alex being involved," replied Rex.

"Has Miss Judy been over?" Anne asked, teasingly.

"Once. Why? Are you jealous?" Rex asked, amused.

"Yes!" replied Anne grinning.

Rex laughed. "So, you going back into hiding, staying for a while, or what? I would like to say you can come to my house, but Judy may drop by unannounced," stated Rex, sadly.

"I don't know. I might spy on Alex Spemann if Hillary doesn't find out, or I might go back into hiding, which I really hate!"

"I can't blame you, I would too! If you decide to spy on Alex, we could go together, if you like. The only thing is we might spy on Alex for days, or even a month or two, and find nothing. How do we prove he's involved with the militia without confronting him?" asked Rex.

"A good question. Even if we confronted him, it's doubtful he'd admit being involved. How else are we going to find out anything? And how safe am I with him around?" asked Anne.

"A good question," admitted Rex.

"You were talking about that shady realty reconstructing those houses on the lower east side, there's a crew there working on the houses," stated Anne.

"I've told the building inspector about that realty and their tactics. I laid it in his lap. It's up to him now," replied Rex.

"Well, it was nice seeing you again. Take care and keep a watch on Hillary as well as Alex, or else you might wish you had," declared Anne. "Say hello to Sgt. Judy for me," teased Anne.

"You take care. I'll keep what you said in mind," replied Rex, grinning.

With that, Anne walked out the door limping as the waiter watched and was gone by the time Rex paid the bill.

A few days later, Hillary called to check with Rex to see if they're still friends or not. Talking to Hillary, Rex conjured up a scheme to see where Hillary stood, as far as Alex Spemann was concerned.

"Anne contacted me by phone. I don't know where she was calling from. Sounded like it was long-distance. She's tired of hiding and being on the run, so she hired me to investigate Alex Spemann to see if he is in with the militia, or just investigating it. She also hired me to discover who else is with the militia. She's still highly suspicious of you as well. She said sometimes people aren't always what they seem to be," stated Rex.

"Oh, so I am to be investigated to see if I am a militia member or a sleeper?" Hillary asked.

"She hired me to investigate Alex Spemann and she doesn't trust you any more than she does the militia," replied Rex. "She gave me money to start, and says if you are so innocent, you won't say a word to Alex Spemann."

"Oh, that makes me so mad she'd suspect me and bring division between you and I. I'm glad she's not around right now!" exclaimed Hillary.

"Well, you did grill me good, which made me wonder, and she immediately became suspicious of you. Then we saw Alex Spemann pull in your driveway," replied Rex. "I understand her suspicions after what she's gone through. As far as you saying you're glad she's not around, if you see her, do not touch or harass her, Captain!"

"Oh, I have the right to question her if I feel the need to, and you can't stop me! I understand what she's been through, but I am not with, or in, the militia in any way!"

"Anne doesn't believe you at all, and grilling me looked suspicious," replied Rex. "Anyway, she has hired me to investigate and says you not saying a word to Alex Spemann will ease her suspicion of you, somewhat. As for questioning Anne, if you have reasons to question her, then, and only then, do you have the right to do so, but nothing more than that. I know the law enough to know that. I'd bet she'd have her lawyer with her at all times, and he'll be a darn good one too; she doesn't leave anything to chance!"

"Oh, I see how it is. So, I'm supposed to let Alex Spemann hang out to dry while you investigate him?" Hillary yelled. I understand her lawyer being present, and I suspect he will be a good one."

"That's pretty much it. I suspect Anne will keep her suspicion about you. It appears you are cozy with Alex, a high person-of-interest."

"I'm a suspect?" Hillary asked, weary.

"Maybe not a suspect, but definitely a person-of-interest to her," replied Rex. "It's almost the same thing!"

"So it is, but Anne feels you brought that on yourself, and I can understand why. If I see the militia knocking on my door, or if they've been in my house, I'll know why."

"You really think I'd do that? You don't know me better than that by now?" Hillary became weary realizing the friendship between himself and Rex was in serious erosion, and, seemingly, there was nothing he could do. Rex had been a friend for many years, as well as a big help in solving crimes.

"I don't know, not now, after seeing you with Alex Spemann," replied Rex.

Hillary realized it was either Alex or Rex, one had become expendable. Was Alex really what Anne suspected? A member or a 'sleeper' of the militia? "Rex, if you think Alex is a part of the militia then I recommend you check him out, and I will keep quiet. But show me something I can believe. I am not a mole of the militia!"

"Okay, Captain, check him out, and if I come up with anything, I'll bring you proof," replied Rex, accepting the challenge.

Hillary knew Rex was dead serious; if there was anything, Rex would find it!

Rex wondered how the realty was doing on the houses, and drove over to the lower east side to see if the crew was there. Pulling up to the curb, there was no sign of the crew, apparently done for the day. Rex looked at the foundation and peeked in the windows. The block foundation seemed to be okay, but time would tell if it stood up in the weather conditions. Peeking in the windows, the walls were plastered well; Rex recognized the brand name of the plaster as being reliable.

Using that plaster, the realty must have gotten the message from the building inspector, "No taking shortcuts or using cheap materials!"

Checking the front and back doors, he noted that both doors were locked. The windows were locked as well, and were excellent quality. There was no way to assess the basement without picking the locks Rex wondered what couldn't be seen from the outside.

Rex called the building inspector. "Jack Owens, this is Rex Morgan. I was wondering if you laid the rules to Brownstone Realty. I was just over at the lower eastside houses area, and the crew working on the houses seems to be doing a pretty good job from the outside. I looked through the windows and the plaster seems to be a quality plaster," stated Rex.

"Good! I told the Brownstone attorneys the crews is to use only top quality brand materials, and if they don't, this department will be on them like fleas on a dog's back!" declared Jack Owens.

"That's good! Sometimes you have to lay down the law with people," replied Rex.

"Well, I was, and they accepted the terms of redeveloping that neighborhood."

"Glad to hear it. That area was an eyesore, but now it will become a nice neighborhood if the families moving in take care of their new homes," replied Rex.

"Oh, being that Berkley Housing Administration is overseeing and allowing needy families to move in, they have to sign a contract to take care of the house and keep it up—yards mowed, no trash piled up in the front or backyard, or junk cars, keep the house decent, no wild, drunken, or drug parties, and no drug operations."

"Oh, alright!" exclaimed Rex. "Well, that's taken care of, so now I have to investigate Alex Spemann, and then I can concentrate on my cases! The only thing I know is to keep doing what I do best and watch where it goes."

Rex drove to Alex Spemann's neighborhood to scan the houses without getting too close. There was a house two blocks away for sale, and Rex pondered if they'd be willing to rent. The house would still belong to the owner, and he'd have an added income. Rex contacted the realty to see. The agent, Nicole Buffington, was reluctant, but said she'd ask the owner and see what the owners, Bill and Coleen Ahlstrom, said.

"You want to rent the house for six months? Why just six months instead of a year or longer?" asked Nicole, puzzled.

"To see if I like the house and neighborhood enough to buy it," replied Rex.

Bill and Coleen Ahlstrom agreed to rent the house for six months at six hundred and twenty dollars a month, with six hundred down as a deposit. Rex paid all utilities plus twenty-five dollars for all overdue payments. Rex agreed, and then rented furniture from *Spit's Rental*.

Rex took casual walks by Alex's house, disguised as an artist out for a stroll. The small camera fastened to Rex's belt, a Nicoma with a 35-90-degree digital lens with a fast shutter speed took good pictures for a small camera.

A couple weeks went by with nothing unusual happening, and then in the middle of the week a late model black Lincoln Continental pulled into Alex's driveway and a couple of business-looking men knocked on Alex's door. Alex let them in. Rex fastened his camera on his belt and walked by Alex's house. As Rex got even across the street from the Lincoln, he clicked the camera, taking a sideview of the car and the license plate. Ducking behind a tree pretending to be resting, Rex waited for the two men to exit the house.

After an hour, the two men came out with Alex standing in the doorway, and they talked a few more minutes. Rex took their pictures as they walked to the car, leaving Alex in the doorway of his house.

I wonder if Anne will recognize these two guys, Rex ponders to himself. *Getting the license number, I can trace the car to see who it belongs to, and what they do. All I have to do is wait for Anne to contact me.*

Rex continued his walk and returned to his house to develop the pictures and contact his friend, Pat Ballenger, a government agent in San Francisco to run the license, and the pictures of the two guys.

It might be good to run a check on Alex Spemann as well. Dianna Sawyer at the license bureau can tell me if these guys are local or not. If Jan Roberts from ABC News or Harold Jabots from NBC News shows up at that rental house, what I'm working on will be exposed for sure! They don't let up until they have their story! I don't think Alex Spemann would appreciate being on the evening news either; he might be expendable with the militia. I wonder how Captain Hillary would feel about that. Upset, I would think, maybe with me for exposing his friend. I wonder if that'd bring him out of the 'sleeper' mode, if he is one.

Four months later, Anne. in disguise as a young girl in pigtails, jeans, and sweatshirt, showed up at Rex's door, catching Rex by surprise. Rex stepped back, letting Anne in while laughing.

"You are full of surprises. You never cease to amaze me; I never know when, where, or what you'll look like next," stated Rex.

"Good, that the way I can keep a eye on you to see what you're up to," replied Anne, laughing.

Rex told Anne about renting the house a couple blocks from Alex Spemann's house and the two men visiting Alex, and then showed Anne their pictures.

Anne studied the pictures intently. "These men, I saw them once or twice where I worked, but I don't know anything about them. They visited Alex Spemann's house? I would've liked to have listened in on their conversation."

"I know a guy who could slip into Alex's house and plant a bug, but anything recorded couldn't be used in court; that's considered 'fruit from the poisonous tree', legally speaking," stated Rex. "It would help knowing whether Alex is a member of the militia or if he is just investigating, as Captain Hillary suggests."

"I don't think Alex is investigating, and I believe your 'Captain Hillary' is covering for him," declared Anne. "I think it would be good to plant a bug in Alex Spemann's house and listen in on his conversations. If he's up to no good, I don't think it'd be wise to play it for your 'Captain Hillary' or not."

"If Captain Hillary is a sleeper or guest, as you suspect, that'd be a way to bring him out in to the open," stated Rex. "You keep referring to him as my 'Captain Hillary'. Yes, we have worked together on cases for some years now. If he's anything like you suspect, I'd expose him to the prosecutor's office in a heartbeat!"

"As for bringing Hillary out in to the open, he might try to silence us quietly and claim it was the militia," replied Anne.

"That blows my mind to think he'd do something like that, or even try!" declared Rex. "I could talk to Larry Flippant, the Director of Internal Affairs, or the new FBI Director, Milton Bradley, have them run a check on Alex Spemann, and tell him you're suspicious of Captain Hillary, but that. by itself, may not be sufficient to run a check."

"That'd be good if he would. I'd feel better and we'd have reason to suspect dear Captain Hillary then."

Anne grinned as Rex shook his head.

Rex kissed Anne on the cheek. "Thank you."

Rex contacted a former client, Leo Espanola, who was good at planting up-to-date electronic bugs in businesses, as well as houses, and arranged for a bug to be planted in Alex's. It could reveal if Alex Spemann was a sleeper or a guest of the militia. Then Rex called the Internal Affairs of the Justice Department for an appointment to talk to Larry Flippant, the receptionist answering the phone.

"I need to talk to Larry Flippant about something that needs to be examined," stated Rex, "as soon as possible."

"Well, let me check with his secretary to see if he's available." After a couple of minutes, the receptionist returns. "Possibly next week he could talk to you," she replied.

"I can't wait that long. I need to talk to him today, or tomorrow at the latest!" exclaimed Rex.

"Hold on a minute then, let me see."

A couple of minutes later, Larry Flippant came on the line and said, "Hello, Rex Morgan. What is so important?"

"I'd rather not talk on the phone. Meet me somewhere safe where we can talk; you'll understand when I see you," stated Rex.

"Is the person-of-interest with you now?" asked Larry.

"Yes," replied Rex.

"I see. Meet me at your favorite club in half an hour," replied Larry Flippant. "Bring this person with you and we can talk."

"Okay," Rex replied, and told Anne.

Anne frowned, becoming nervous. "Here we go again. Will it ever stop?" Anne flared.

"Hopefully, yes, but when, I can't say," replied Rex.

Anne dressed as the young girl again in pigtails, jeans, and sweatshirt.

Rex and Anne drove to the club and went inside as the valet parked Rex's car. Waiting inside for a few minutes, Rex saw Larry Flippant come in looking around for Rex. He then spots Rex.

"This is the person-of-interest? She looks like a young schoolgirl. You robbing the cradle, Rex?" Larry teased. "Going after underage girls is illegal, and you know that."

"I like em' young and pretty," Rex joked back.

Anne sat there grinning.

"So, I see! So, I see! Okay, Rex, what is so important that it can't wait?" asked Larry Flippant.

"Captain Hillary grilled me a while back as to where Anne Towers is hiding and I told him she keeps moving around, but he continued to ask. Later, he said Alex Spemann requested Hillary question me about Anne's whereabouts," stated Rex. "I told Anne about it and she suggested we check Alex Spemann out and see if anyone from the militia showed up at Captain Hillary's house. Seeing Alex, she gets really nervous, I mean really nervous! She said she had seen him at the Militia's Militia headquarters where she worked at the time."

"Is this true? You actually saw Alex Spemann at the militia building where you worked at the time?" asked Larry Flippant, alarmed while looking at Anne.

"Yes, I saw him a number of times. I didn't hear what he and the militia staff were saying because I was in my office while they were across the hall. To go over there snooping, I'd have been noticed and that wouldn't have been good!" stated Anne nervously.

"Just recently, I rented a house a couple blocks from Alex Spemann's house, and there were two men in a black Lincoln Continental in his driveway who knocked on his door. Alex let them in, they stayed for an hour, and then left. I took their pictures with Alex at his talking to them and getting into their car. I got their license plate number."

Larry looked at the pictures and put them in his coat pocket, not knowing what to say.

"I saw those men at the militia headquarters, but I don't know who they are or what they do," stated Anne.

"I'll look into this and see what comes up. If Alex Spemann is involved, he'll be charged with associating with a subversive group, but he is a big-time lawyer in the Justice Department," stated Larry Flippant, still surprised.

"When I told Captain Hillary Anne saw Alex at the militia building, Hillary suggested that Alex must be investigating," stated Rex.

"We'll see where Alex stands with the Militia's Militia, and whether he's investigating or being a mole in the Justice Department!" declared Larry Flippant.

With that clear, they had lunch and left, Larry Flippant looked at Anne, grinned, and shook his head Anne grinned back.

Rex and Anne returned to Rex's house. Rex, without saying anything to Anne, watched if anyone was following them, but saw no one.

Well, Captain Hillary, this is taken care of. Now we'll see if Alex Spemann is a good or a bad guy!

"You staying for a cookout and evening together?" Rex asked late that afternoon. "Maybe stay the night as well?"

"Hum, that sounds interesting and exciting," Anne replied with a big hug and a long, intimate kiss.

Rex and Anne had a romantic evening: a cookout, relaxing in the porch swing for a couple of hours before watching TV, and thenmaking their way to the bedroom.

The next morning Rex and Anne came down in robes and had breakfast out on the deck.

"It's so pleasant sitting out here, so relaxing and soothing," Anne commented. "I just wish I could say that about my house over there," she said, looking next door.

"Yeah, I sure enjoy my house and deck a lot. I come out here when I'm depressed," replied Rex. "I imagine you miss your house; it's really a nice house. I can understand."

Rex and Anne went back inside for a playful, romantic romp, then shower and get dressed.

"I want to go over and just look around," mourned Anne.

"You could, but you might be miserable afterward," replied Rex.

"You're right, I would."

"Maybe after all this is over and those moles and sleepers are caught, then you could go over there," suggested Rex.

"If they're ever caught!" snared Anne. "How will I ever know?"

"That's hard to say. When you're out in public and see one, get on your cellphone and call the police or the FBI," replied Rex. "I could check if it's possible for you to carry a gun for protection under your circumstances of having to be on the move."

"You think they would allow me to carry a gun?" asked Anne hopefully.

"I don't know, but I could check."

With that said, Rex called Wayne Milton, the Berkley Police Commissioner, to inquire over a gun permit for Anne.

"Under the circumstances, I think it would be possible, if she's in fear for her life," replied Wayne Milton. "However, she'd should make sure it was a matter of life and death, and be able to prove it, if necessary."

Rex told Wayne Milton about Captain Hillary grilling him about where Anne was, and then afterward said Alex Spemann requested him to. "Anne and I went over and staked out Captain Hillary's house. Upon seeing Alex, Anne became nervous, saying she had seen him various times at the Militia's Militia building, where she worked at the time."

Hearing this, Wayne Milton became alarmed there might be another militia mole or sleeper trying to get at Anne. "Captain Hillary grilled you on Anne's whereabouts because Alex Spemann requested it?"

"Yes, sir, that's what Hillary said," Rex replied. "I've told Larry Flippant, Director of Internal Affairs, and the FBI Director, Milton Bradley, about it. They are looking into it to discover why Alex Spemann would want to know where Anne was after all this time."

"I'll have to check with Flippant and Milton Bradley to see what they've come up with and where we go from here. You think Captain Hillary might be involved with Spemann and the militia?" Wayne asked stunned.

"I'm don't know. Hillary and I have worked together for years, but I can't say, one way or the other, but it might have been because Alex Spemann requested it," replied Rex.

"True, you have been friends for some time now. Under these circumstances, I'd say it would be okay for Anne to have a permit to carry a gun, but only for her protection."

"I understand, and she will too," replied Rex.

Rex relayed Wayne Milton's message to Anne, and she was relieved.. She fixed her make-up and clothes to look like a high-class business woman.

"Wow, you've really changed your disguise," remarked Rex as they entered the car.

They went to City Hall to apply for a permit, and then the police station to turn in the permit. Anne's fingerprints and photo were already on file. Rex waited in the visitors' lounge and watched to see if Hillary would recognize Anne, and then come out to see who she was.

Hillary, while in his office on the phone, looked up and saw Anne. Hillary came out to see if it was really her. "Is that you, Anne Towers? What are you doing here, if I may ask?"

Sgt. Judy Sturgis looked from her desk with a sour expression. "She's getting a permit to carry a gun, a .357 magnum," replied Officer Susan Hayman.

"You need a gun? Rex told me you suspected me. I am not the bad guy, but under the circumstances, I guess I can understand."

"Rex told me how you grilled him over my whereabouts, and then you said Alex Spemann requested it, but I wonder about VOW," declared Anne. "Rex saw two questionable characters enter Alex Spemann's house! He's a friend of yours, you say. That makes me wonder about you even more! You stay away from me. If want to question me, it will be with my attorney present! Otherwise, you and Alex Spemann stay away from me!"

"Okay,I understand, but I don't mean you any harm," stammered Hillary.

Sgt. Judy Sturgis and Officer Susan Hayman watched and listened in shock that their captain was being talked to in this way.

"I don't believe you!"

"Okay."

With that, Anne stormed out of the police station as Hillary, Sgt. Judy, and Officer Susan stood, still stunned, and then Hillary returned to his office to make a call.

Rex, watching through the lounge window, figured, *Yep, Hillary's calling Alex Spemann to let him know Anne is in town.*

Hillary continued to sit at his desk looking over some papers after the phone call. Rex went outside, joining Anne as they walked to his car, a block away, while talking.

"You left, and Hillary went back to his office and made a phone call, and I think I know to who," Rex tells Anne. "Sgt. Judy Sturgis and Officer Susan Hayman were watching in total shock at you coming down on their captain. I could hear you clearly in the visitors' lounge, and I think everybody there heard you."

"Good, maybe they'll know what kind of captain they have," replied Anne laughing.

"Now do you believe me?"

"I don't know if he called Alex, but I'd say it's a safe bet. What do you say we go to Wayne Milton's office to let him know?" suggested Rex.

"Yeah, then he can start an inquiry on your Captain Hillary," replied Anne teasingly.

"After working with the captain for many years, it's still hard for me to imagine him being involved in something like that."

At Wayne Milton's office, the secretary announced Rex and Anne's arrival. Wayne ushered them into his office.

"You must be Anne Towers," inquired Wayne.

"Yes, I am."

"Sir, Anne went to the City Hall for a permit for a handgun, then took the application to the police station, and Captain Hillary saw Anne and came out to meet her. Anne ordered him and Alex Spemann to stay away from her. After Anne left, Hillary went back in his office and made a phone call," stated Rex. "I suspect it was to Alex Spemann to let him know Anne is in town, but I have no way of knowing."

"That's interesting, sort of brings Captain Hillary into the picture as a person-of-interest, doesn't it?" stated Wayne Milton. "I heard how you, Anne, came down on him; he's not used to a woman calling him out like that, especially in front of his staff. It embarrassed him."

Anne just smiled.

"Yeah, I'd say it brings him into the spotlight," replied Rex.

"Lay a trap for Alex Spemann and Captain Hillary, I'd say," replied the Police Commissioner. "I'll request a couple of officers to tail both Alex Spemann and Captain Hillary to see where they go and who they see. It may not be safe to stay at your house just yet, but, on the other hand, the honey draws the bees."

"Are you suggesting we return to my house to draw the militia to my house and take a chance of getting it shot up?" asked Rex anxiously.

"I'll have some plainclothes officers follow and see you safely inside, and then they'll wait to see what happens. If the militia shows up, then we'd have reason to bring Captain Hillary and Alex Spemann in for questioning," stated the Police Commissioner. "But why are they making a move on you after all of this time has passed?" Wayne asked, looking at Anne. "Has something new come up?"

"Not that I know of, other than wanting to even the score," replied Anne. "Possible."

Anne suggested the officers wait inside her house next door to Rex as well as outside, but they should park the cars down the street so the militia wouldn't suspect anything. Wayne Milton liked that idea.

The first few nights nothing happened. Then one late afternoon, an old, beat-up, yellow car with two men with hats pulled over their eyes slowly drove by Anne's and Rex's houses, turned around two blocks, returned slowly, and then drove away, probably casing Rex's house and deciding what to do.

"Well, they probably remember the last raid on my house. We were waiting for them; they won't make the same mistake twice," stated Rex.

"The cat and mouse game all over again," replied Anne angrily.

That evening, Leo Espanola called. "I have a recording of Alex Spemann talking about a lot of little things with Captain Hillary, that may not mean anything, but there are a couple of calls from a man called Benxi that may sound interesting, if you can follow their conversation; some off-the-wall ramblings about something or other. I couldn't make sense of it."

"Hold onto it. I'll try to make sense of it. If I can't, maybe Anne, the Police Commissioner, or the FBI Director can," replied Rex. "I really appreciate you doing this. I owe you a big favor."

"Do you recognize the name, Benxi?" Rex asked Anne.

Anne thought for a moment, and then unsure, replied that she had heard the name mentioned once or twice, but couldn't connect it to anyone important, or his personal standing with the militia.

"Well, a former client I hired to bug Alex's house just called to say Alex Spemann talked with Captain Hillary about things, that may not mean anything, but a man named Bennie talked to Alex about something that may sound interesting if we can follow their conversation, a bit off-the-wall rambling," stated Rex.

"I'd like to listen. Maybe I could make sense of it," replied Anne.

"Wayne Milton, Milton Bradley, and Larry Flippant would like to sit in with you and make sense of it, I'm sure."

"Give them a call then," replied Anne.

Rex called Wayne Milton and explained the situation at Alex's house.

"You had a former client bug Alex Spemann's house? We can't mention or use it in court because you did it on your own. It's called 'fruit of the poisonous tree', and we can't use anything related to it. It might let us know if Alex Spemann is a militia member or a sleeper, though," stated Wayne Milton.

"Under those circumstance, do you want to hear the tape or not?" asked Rex.

"Yes, I want to hear the tape, and I'd like Anne to explain the rambling, if it means anything to her," said Wayne.

"Larry Flippant and Milton Bradley would probably like to hear it as well," stated Rex.

"Yeah, I think they would. I'll give them a call while you get the tape and come to my office," replied Wayne.

Rex drove over to Leo Espanola's house to obtain the tape, arriving in a middle-to low-income neighborhood. Leo asked Rex to check out his brother-in-law, in exchange for his bugging Alex's house.

"I suspect my low-down brother-in-law is cheating on my sister; he doesn't come straight home two or three nights a week. He gets home about three hours late, saying he worked overtime, but my sister called his job, and they said he had left at the end of his shift," stated Leo.

"Okay, follow him and see where he goes," said Rex. "Where does he work? I need a recent picture and a description of him as well."

"He works at the Fulton Foundry," replied Leo. "He works days, 7:00 A.M. to 5:00 P.M. He is about 5'9" or 5'10" and weighs about 190-200 pounds with brown hair," he said, handing Rex a picture of his brother-in-law. His name is Harry Hickman."

Rex returned to his car to study Harry's picture. Being a cheater, Anne was repulsed. Within a few minutes, Rex returned home to make a copy of the tape, and bound it on the backside of his bed's headboard. Rex called Wayne Milton, letting him know he had the tape and asked, "Where do you want us to meet?"

"Come to my office. Larry Flippant and Milton Bradley want to listen to the tape and want Anne to explain if she can," stated Wayne.

"Okay, I'll tell her."

Rex told Anne, and she prepared her disguise, to be on the safe side, and they left for Director Wayne Milton's office.

Arriving at the director's office, Rex and Anne were directed to the District Attorney's conference room. They were surprised to see Assistant District Attorney Cheryl Nickels there, as well as Wayne, Larry Flippant, and Milton Bradley.

"Well, I see everybody is here," declared Anne nervously.

"This is a serious matter; a justice department official is in question of being a person-of-interest in a subversive organization," stated the Director of Internal Affairs, Larry Flippant.

"So, it is. Let's listen to the tape and then decide," replied Rex. "I realize this can't be mentioned or used in court, but the information might be helpful."

"First of all, you hired a former client to electronically bug Alex Spemann's house?" asked Assistant District Attorney, Cheryl Nickels.

"Yes, Anne recognized Alex Spemann at the Militia's Militia building many times, and seeing him at Captain Hilary's house, she became extremely nervous," stated Rex Morgan. "Working in her office across the hall, she couldn't hear what was said, but she saw Alex Spemann shake hands with the top staff, and then enter one of the staff's offices with them! To go snooping and listening, she would be in grave danger!"

"I can understand Anne being nervous, but this is a very serious matter," stated Cheryl Nickels.

"I understand. but I know and remember what I saw!" declared Anne. "Why he was there each time, I don't know, but, like Rex said, snooping around and listening would have been very dangerous!"

"This tape may help to reveal if Alex Spemann is a member, a sleeper, or whatever his business there was," declared Rex. "What do you say we listen and see?"

"Play the tape and maybe it will reveal something," suggested Wayne Milton.

Rex turned the tape on and they listened. After it finished, Rex turned it off to hear the officials' comments.

"Could you understand what they were talking about?" Wayne looked at Cheryl, Milton, and Larry, confused, but they're confused as well. The four looked at Anne to explain.

"They were talking in coded riddles, but I think I was able to make out most, or some of it, anyway. They do that on the phone as a safety precaution in case the line is tapped," stated Anne. "They are a very suspicious group; they are always suspicious of outsiders!"

"Can you explain it then?" asked Cheryl Nickels.

"They were talking about money and stock certificates transfers to a Columbian bank deposit, and they suspect a snitch is among them, and wonder who it could be. They suspect it's someone they trust, someone of position in the group. If there is and they find out who, I wouldn't want to be them! They use the Gestapo methods, I've heard. People disappear!" exclaimed Anne, nervously.

"They aren't nice people, we already know that. So, Alex Spemann is a person-of-interest in a subversive organization." stated Larry Flippant, disgusted, as well as Milton Bradley, Cheryl, and Wayne as they shook their heads in disbelief.

"Them not being nice people is putting it mildly." stated Anne firmly. "I'd like this tape to be confirmed before you take it at face value, but this is only my understanding of this tape."

"We'll want to analyze it before taking any action, but it puts Alex Spemann in a bad predicament, and makes him a suspect for sure," stated Larry Flippant. "With this tape being obtained illegally, we can't use it to hold Alex Spann, but it lets us know about him. If the militia finds out we know about him, Alex will be expendable. We could use that to confront him and get a confession."

"If you do go after Alex Spemann, it'd be best to put him in immediate custody because if the militia gets wind of this, he's a goner for sure! The militia won't mess around!" stated Anne.

"You think we should talk to him or have you confront him in person?" asked Cheryl Nickels.

"Well, I didn't say anything about confronting him. He might recognize me and become belligerent. I don't know about that," replied Anne.

"You could remain disguise and hide until we actually have him in person, and then you will be protected," stated Wayne Milton. "He'll be taken into custody while here."

"If you go to his house and there's someone there, or anywhere around, watching, they will know something's up," stated Rex. "The jig will be up then, to be on the safe side."

"We could tell him we have a matter in which we need his input and have him come here," suggested Milton Bradley, "and take him into custody when he gets here."

"That would be safer for him than going to his house," stated Rex.

Anne nodded in agreement.

It was setup; Rex and Anne would stay in the next room until they actually had Alex Spemann in Wayne Melton's office, then, and only then, would Anne confront him.

"Alex, Wayne Milton, and Larry Flippant have a complex legal problem that might have to go to the state court to settle, and Wayne suggested you might be able to work something out. He doesn't want to discuss it over the phone for security reasons. I can't understand his problem, so he figures you might. He feels you'll be able to understand whatever it is puzzling him," stated Cheryl Nickels.

"Sure, I'll come there now," Alex replied with pride that someone again needed his input on an important legal matter. *When things get complex or technical, they call on me, Alex Spemann!*

Alex arrived at Wayne Milton's office ready to solve a complex legal question or technical issue. Wayne Milton sat at his desk with Cheryl standing beside him, looking at some papers and a tape recorder. Milton Bradley sat in a chair looking on. After Alex entered, Larry Flippant rose from a chair and closed the door.

"What's the problem, Wayne?" Alex asked, expecting to solve a problem.

"I have something I'd like you to listen to and explain, Alex. It's too jumbled for me," said Wayne, turning on the tape.

Hearing the tape, Alex became alarmed, and looked around nervously. He asked, "What is this? Where did you get that?" Alex bellowed, realizing he had fallen into a trap.

"What's the matter? What's wrong? We need you to explain this tape. We got it from your house. We are unable to use it in court, but we know all about you now, and there is someone we'd like you to meet. She recognizes you as the guest at the Militia's Militia where she used to work, Anne Towers!"

With that, Rex and Anne stepped in from the other room, catching Alex by surprise. Alex became shaky and started to sweat. Wayne turned on the tape recorder to record everything said.

"Hello, Alex. I saw you at various times at the Militia's Militia building shaking hands with the top militia staff," declared Anne.

"I don't recognize you; I have never seen you before!" stammered Alex in panic.

"Oh, that's because I had an office across the hall from the staff offices. I had no reason to be over there without being noticed, and that would've been horrible for me, and you know all about that!"

"What's the matter, Alex? You seem panicky. You nervous after hearing the tape and seeing Anne?" taunted Milton.

"What is the matter?" Larry Flippant studied Alex quietly.

"I..." stammered Alex.

"You tell us what you know about the Militia's Militia and it will go a lot easier for you. We'll put you in protective custody," stated Milton Bradley. "But if you don't cooperate, oh well. This tape being obtained illegally, we can't hold you by it alone, but if we know about you, how long do you think it will take the militia to find out we know? However, Rex Morgan traced the two suspects who visited you, and found them to be members of the militia. We can use that to hold and charge you! That will make you expendable with the militia! Do you want a lawyer? You're entitled to a lawyer. Maybe Anne can help us with disguises, but only if you cooperate. She is great at disguises! What do you say?"

Alex Spemann broke down, saying the militia would kill him for sure, and realizing his predicament, a lawyer would draw attention to him, which would eventually get back to the militia.

Anne said she could help with disguises. Alex, after regaining his composure, agreed to cooperate, told what was on the tape while being recorded.

"There is a snitch in the group, but the militia doesn't know who. They want to make a money transfer and send stock certificates to a Columbian bank deposit."

That was what Anne had said.

Alex said if the snitch was caught, they would disappear in the most unimaginable way. Anne agreed. Alex then explained what he knew about the militia, and what he had done with them. Alex said he didn't know what world banks the militia did business with; only the top brass knew that.

"What about Captain Hillary? Is he a member or a sleeper?" Rex asked.

"No, we grew up together and went to the Police Academy, but Hillary is just a close friend—a straight guy."

Rex felt relieved as Anne looked at Rex with a knowing smile.

"Hillary's a straight guy as far as you know, right?" asked Anne, still not convinced of Hillary's innocence.

"Oh, I'm sure he's as clean as a whistle," replied Alex. "Of course, there are rumors of 'deep sleepers' who only the top brass knows about."

Rex looked at Alex, alarmed at the thought of Hillary being deep sleeper.

"Did you request Hillary to question Rex as to my whereabouts?" continued Anne. By now, Wayne Melton, Cheryl Nickels, Milton Bradley, and Larry Flippant listened intently.

"Well, let's see…I did ask if Rex knew where you were, but I didn't request Hillary to question him," replied Alex.

"Are you sure about that?" cut in Rex, angry at the thought of Captain Hillary grilling him while being a deep sleeper.

"Best I remember is I asked Hillary if you knew where Anne was, but Hillary might have misunderstood that I wanted him to question you," stated Alex. "Are you wondering about Hillary?" asked Alex alarmed. "As far as I know, he's clean."

"In that case, I suggest we all go over to Rex's house and invite Hillary over for a cookout," suggested Cheryl.

Rex, in shock, agreed while Anne looked on silently. Cheryl, Wayne, Larry, Milton, with Alex in custody, Rex, and Anne arrived at Rex's house. Cheryl, Wayne, Larry, Milton, and Anne wait as Rex invited Hillary over for a cookout, and then ducked into bedrooms.

"Hey, Captain, this is Rex. How about coming over for a cookout? My brother-in-law has a legal problem and he wants to know where he stands with the law. I'm not sure on it," lied Rex.

"Oh, are we still friends? If he has a legal problem, why not bring him here?" asked Hillary.

"I thought we could patch things up and be friends again," replied Rex. "Maybe have a cookout?"

"Okay, Rex, I'll be over. It sure is good to hear your voice again," replied Hillary, happy, but cautious.

Hillary arrived shortly, happy to be friends with Rex again. After getting inside, Alex Spemann stepped out to greet Hillary, surprising him.

"Hey, Rex said nothing about you being here." said Hillary suspiciously.

"Rex tells me you said I requested you to question if he knew where Anne was. I asked you if Rex knew, but I don't recall requesting you grill him relentlessly," stated Alex.

"I misunderstood you, honest! Is this why you invited me over here, Rex?"

"I asked you over so the two of you could get your story straight." stated Rex.

Hillary went to leave, but Rex tugged at his arm. "What's the matter? Don't you want to get this straightened out?" inquired Rex.

"I…better go," stammered Hillary. "You owe me an explanation, Captain."

"I'm sorry, Rex. I am truly sorry," stammered Hillary as he attempted to leave but Rex continued to tug at his arm.

Cheryl, Wayne, Larry, and Anne stayed in hiding, but watched and listened intently. Rex released Hillary's arm, allowing him to leave, then they stepped out.

"It's hard to say whether he's involved or not. We'll have to tail his every move and get a court order for a phone tap," stated Larry Flippant looking at Rex.

"I'd say he's definitely a person-of-interest in being a suspected militia sleeper, or used to be," stated Cheryl.

Rex felt let down, hoping Hillary would be clean of any wrongdoing. He began to wonder when Hillary grilled him, but still hoped.

Everyone decided to have a cookout to ease the tension. Anne instructed Alex in the art of disguise, and how to not stand out in public.

"I understand," replied Alex.

"Well, that's over, but I still wonder about your Captain Hillary," Anne commented to Rex.

"We'll find out about him; we'll keep tab to see if he's clean or dirty," stated Wayne Milton. "You're good at that, will you work with us?"

"I wouldn't mind tailing him to clear my mind," replied Rex.

"Good."

"In a way, I have a good mind to move back into my house and enjoy it. If the militia comes, I now have a registered .357 magnum to protect me!" stated Anne. "Besides, Rex lives right next door."

"I'm sure you've missed that house. I know I would!" declared Cheryl Nickels. "That's a nice house, and so is Rex's! I can see why Sgt. Judy Sturgis is interested in Rex with a nice house like this!"

Rex grinned and looked at Anne. They all went out on the deck to grill and relax.

Captain Hillary realized his predicament with Rex, Anne, and maybe Assistant District Attorney Cheryl Nickels, Police Commissioner Wayne Milton, FBI Director Milton Bradley, and the local Director of Internal Affairs Larry Flippant if Rex had said anything to suspect him of being a militia member. The truth was he used to be a sleeper in the militia, but not anymore.

How do I prove I am no longer am? Even Alex Spemann didn't know, but probably wonder now. What am I to do? Level with them? I could lose my career, my pension, and be charged as well! Hillary took a stress pill and pondered whether to call Rex and confide in him to see what he thought he should do, but over the phone?

Later that day, Hillary arrived at Rex's house to level with him. It appeared only Rex was at home. Knocking, Rex answered.

"Rex, I need to talk to you, but I didn't want to do it over the phone," Hillary declared.

"Okay, talk." Rex stepped back, allowing Hillary to come in and be greeted by Anne.

"Hi, Hillary," said Anne.

Hillary wasn't surprised to see Anne. "I need to talk to Rex alone," Hillary replied.

"It's okay. We can talk with Anne here. I don't think your returning really surprised her," stated Rex.

"Okay then, I used to be a militia sleeper, but I'm done with that now. Alex Spemann didn't know because he wasn't supposed to know," stated Hillary.

"I wondered about you after you grilled me. Alex says he didn't request that. So why did you grill me?"

"I misunderstood Alex, thinking he had requested it," replied Hillary.

"I'm supposed to believe that?" Rex asked.

Anne looked on in disbelief.

"That is the honest-to-God's truth!" Hillary declared.

"Well, I think you need to explain it to the three who was just here; they heavily suspect you anyway, and they're going to be on you like fleas on a dog's back,!" stated Rex.

"I suspected that after I left," replied Hillary. "I'll lose my career, my pension, and face the possibility of being charged!"

"Very possible," replied Rex. "Very possible, indeed, but if you confess everything you know and did, they might go easy on you."

"I face the possibility of the militia coming after me, as well," stated Hillary.

"I can help you with disguises until they move you to a safe place," stated Anne. "You're good at that; on the street, I never recognized you," replied Hillary.

"That's the intention!" Anne said.

Rex called Wayne Milton and told him Hillary had confessed about his involvement with the militia. Wayne said to bring him in.

Arriving at Wayne's office, Cheryl Nickels, Larry Flippant, Milton Bradley, and a stenographer was there. as well. The tape recorder was on and the stenographer typed as Captain Hillary stated his name as requested, then described his involvement with the militia.

"How many more sleepers do you know of, or think there might be?" asked Cheryl Nickels.

"I have no way of knowing; only the top brass knows that," replied Hillary.

"They are in prison," stated Wayne Milton.

"Yes, but I'd say the second or third in command has taken over. As to how effective they are, I don't know," replied Hillary. "They may decide to lay low for a while. You practically put them out of business."

"Not entirely, they still have money and stock certificates stashed in banks in third world countries that have no treaty with the U.S., so we can't touch that," stated Larry Flippant.

"I don't know anything about that; I was never privileged on the business of the militia. Only the top brass knew. You really have to be important to know anything at all about them!" stated Hillary. I knew very little about the staff in prison, as well—very little. That's how they played it."

Anne agreed.

"Since you are no longer in the militia, so you say, and not knowing much about them, it's up to the District Attorney where to go from here. We need to stay in touch with you, and if we have any more questions we'll contact you," stated Wayne Milton.

"You had to be pretty high up to know anything about the brass, especially the top," declared Anne.

Cheryl, Wayne, and Larry listened, making no comments.

"What about my career and pension?" Hillary asked, scared of losing everything he had worked hard for.

"I'd say you need to take a leave of absence, but stick around until we decide how far to take this. The fact that you haven't been in the militia for some time is in your favor, but I don't know yet. We'll keep you informed, but you must stay put, and not try to run," stated Cheryl Nickels.

The stenographer left with her machine to record and file it.

"Anne is good at that. I wouldn't know where to start," stated Hillary.

"Who will take over while you're on a leave of absence? Who's your second-in-command?" asked Wayne Milton.

"I'd say Eric Wilkson; he's a bit high-strung, but a good guy. He believes the police can solve their own cases without outside help. We used to argue about that," stated Hillary.

"In that case, I can concentrate on my own cases as I get them and have more time for fun," stated Rex.

Anne agreed.

"Oh, I figured he might come around for help eventually, if he gets into a case he can't solve," replied Hillary. "My job will be a whole different field of work for him. I pretty much made decisions, sometimes with your help, but making the big decisions will be entirely new to him."

"On the job training, huh?" asked Larry Flippant, amused. "It might be good for him; a valuable experience."

"What am I going to do with all that free time? I'm not used to that," stated Hillary.

"Develop a hobby, something you enjoy like working on a craft, playing on the computer, volunteering your time, or catching up on things," replied Anne.

"I owe a former client a favor; he planted the bug in Alex's house for me," stated Rex. "I need to do some detective work for him and see where it goes. He can't do it himself, and he's too close to be involved. That is, if we're all through here."

With that said, Rex left to go home for his camera, and Anne went to her house while Rex leaves for Fulton Foundry before the brother-in-law, Harry Hickman got off work. Rex got to the foundry ten minutes before the workers came out and parked close to the exit gate. Rex mad sure his camera was ready.

Harry came out and moved over to a female worker's car to talk to her, and Rex took their picture. Harry talking to her didn't prove anything, but it may later if there were more convincing pictures.

Harry, on the way to his car, followed her to. Harry parked next to her car, and they went to room seven on the ground floor as Rex snapped their picture at the door, and again as they entered the room. Rex took a picture of their cars parked at the motel as well. Rex waited until they left two and half hours later. Again, Rex took their picture coming out with his arm around her, snuggling.

Rex continued the stake outs that whole week, as well as the following two weeks: taking pictures, recording the date and time for each picture. When the pictures were developed, Rex wrote the date and time on the back of each picture.

Rex called Leo Espanola to notify him that he got the pictures. Leo was mostly glad, but sad it might hurt his sister, Mariana, and break up her marriage.

"This makes my planting the bug in Alex's house paid in full," stated Leo.

"I'm glad I could help you, but it might break up a marriage," replied Rex. "I'm home, and my favor to Leo is paid," stated Rex, arriving back home.

"Good," replied Anne.

"I wonder what Eric Wilkson is like," commented Rex to Anne later that afternoon.

"I'm sure we will find out," replied Anne.

Soon to find out, both Rex and Anne!

Eric Wilkson was sworn in as the new police chief and things were set to Eric's taste. Hillary's fixtures that were left behind were stored in the basement Rex received a call from the new police chief.

"Rex, if you and Anne Towers could come to my office for a meeting, I would appreciate it," stated Eric Wilkson.

"Meeting about what?" asked Rex, a bit confused.

"The new setup here, now that I'm the chief."

"Couldn't you tell us over the phone? I have a speaker." Rex said, alarmed.

"Well, yeah, but I'd like for us to get acquainted as well," stated Eric.

"Okay…" replied Rex, still confused.

Rex and Anne arrived at the police headquarters and were ushered into the new chief's office. Sgt. Judy made herself busy shuffling papers at a cabinet against the wall.

"I'm glad both of you could come. Whenever a new official takes office they usually have their own way of doing and running things to their taste," stated Eric.

"I understand, and I'm sure Anne does too," declared Rex.

Anne nodded in agreement.

"Good, I understand Hillary depended on you to help on some cases, and even doing investigative undercover work for him, but I feel I can handle my own cases and undercover work on my own. If I should need help, I have paid officers here who can help me if I should need them," stated Eric in an arrogant declaration of independence. "This may be new to me, but I feel I can handle it."

"Oh, I see, well, in that case, I can fully concentrate on my cases and enjoy my home," declared Rex in surprise at such a rude rebut from the new chief.

Anne stated she could enjoy her home as well. "Well, he certainly let us know where we stand!" declared Anne in anger on the way to the car.

"Yeah, he did. If he ever does need help, I will be unavailable with my cases to help him in any way!" declared Rex, annoyed.

"I can't blame you, I'll will be too busy too," added Anne.

Rex decided to let Hillary know what the new chief said by driving to Hillary's house. Hillary, hearing Eric's arrogant rebut to Rex and Anne, laughed and said that soundede like him.

"He always thought I depended on you too heavily in tough cases instead of working it out on my own. In a couple of cases, I tried to work it out with the staff's help and it was thrown out at court unsolved and can't be retried because of Double Jeopardy. That should have told him something, but he just shook it off," stated Hillary. He feels if the police can't solve a case, it can't be solved and it would be a reflection on the police to hire outside help."

"Well, if he ever needs help, I'll be too busy to give advice or help, way too busy!" declared Rex.

"Me too," Anne said.

"You're going to let him squirm in quicksand if he gets into trouble, or has a case he can't solve?" Hillary asked, laughing.

"That's right; let him work out of his own mess, sink, swim, or drown!" declared Rex.

Anne nodded in agreement. Hillary continued laughing, realizing Eric may regret his bold declaration and one day be in serious trouble. "They may bring you back as chief if he falls flat on his face and embarrasses the police force," stated Rex.

"That would be funny. I've been through with the militia many years, and I didn't do much when I was with them, but to be asked to come back would be a face-saver and the highlight of my career!" declared Hillary. The second-in-command under Eric would be a weak knee, easygoing flunky! I think I'll let them beg me to come back!"

"I can't blame you there," Rex replied, laughing.

"I have moved back into my house; it's too much to give up, and I enjoy my home." declared Anne.

"I can't blame you. You both have nice homes, better than I can afford!" replied Hillary. "I'm comfortable in my house; it's nice and what I can afford, but it doesn't compare to either one of your houses."

"The important thing is if you're comfortable where you live, the taxes, insurance, and maintenance can be a bit of an expense," stated Rex.

"Yeah, I imagine it is, more than I could afford!" replied Hillary.

On the way home, Rex said he intended to see if Mr. Eric Wilkson could make it on his own, or even with the squad's help.

You're in for it now, Eric, Anne though to herself.

As fate would have it, soon Wayne Milton would have no choice but to ask Hillary to return as Police Chief with a raise and more benefits, but now running the police force was in the hands of Eric Wilkson. If Hillary returned as Police Chief, Rex figured Wayne Milton would probably give Eric Wilkson a good pension.

Sure enough, three months later a kidnapping took place; one of the city's most prominent residents, twenty-three-year-old, Frieda Schumacher, had disappeared and hadn't been seen for three days. On the fourth day, her father, Karl Schumacher, received a ransom for one million dollars if he wished to see his daughter alive again. The note said he would be told later how and where to deliver the money. The note was on plain, white printer paper with no watermark that could be bought anywhere with regular computer print. It was left in his mail slot. He wasn't to contact the authorities, but the housekeeper did anyway, thinking she was doing the right thing.

"They didn't leave directions as to when, how, or where it was to be delivered?" Eric asked Karl.

"No. I suppose they'll tell me later how it's to be delivered," replied Karl, worried.

The mother, Gertrud, sat on the couch wringing her hands in a state of stress.

"We'll get a couple of detectives here with a device to trace the calls connected to your phone in case they call," stated Eric.

"The ransom note said no contact with the authorities!" exclaimed Karl.

"Yes, but we were called and we're here now, which they probably know by now," stated Eric Wilkson.

"What if they don't call?"

"Oh, I think they will in some way or other if they want the money."

Another note was discovered in the mail slot, apparently delivered sometime during the night. The note read:

You were not to call the police, but you did anyway! Oh well… BYE!

Neither the first nor the second note contained fingerprints, and were printed on the same type of paper.

Three weeks went by with no contact, and then another three weeks, but still no response. Karl and Gertrud both felt they'd never see their daughter again. Eric posted information and a description about the daughter, but nobody came forward. Karl posted a $100,000 reward for information on who kidnapped Frieda Schumacher in the newspaper, television, and on the Internet, but nothing yielded a response.

The neighbors were questioned if they saw any strange cars driving by, or strangers hanging around the Schumacher's house, but no one saw anything. Someone had to know Frieda and her family, but who'd kidnap the daughter? Someone who had a grudge against Karl or Gertrud and want to hurt them? Someone who had a grudge against Frieda? Three former clients were questioned, but it went nowhere.

Eric was stumped; the detectives had no clues or leads, a total dead-end. Eric looked at the family-friends, but came up empty and, instead, decided to investigate who had dealings with the family. No luck. Eric studied Karl and Gertrud and the housekeeper, but still no luck. *What do I do?* Eric wondered. *Hillary would call Rex Morgan, but I have declared the police don't any need help; we can solve our own cases without outside assistance. To call on Rex now would be a bad reflection on me!*

Another two weeks went by, but still nothing turned up. It looked like the daughter had disappeared with no trace. Eric realized he had no choice but to swallow his pride, call Rex, and ask if he'd take the case. Eric called, but there was no answer. Eric left a message that he needed Rex's help; he was stumped with no leads as to where Frieda was.

Two days later, Rex called the police station and a desk clerk answered the phone.

"Is the chief there? He called requesting my help on a case, but I'm way too busy another one," stated Rex. "He told Anne and I he could solve his own, and, if need be, he had the paid staff to help him," stated Rex.

"I'll relay the message to him," replied the clerk.

Eric, hearing the message, grunted. *Rex is leaving me to squirm in my own quicksand because I made that declaration! Stumped as Mal la do!*

"Hey, Captain Hillary, how are you doing?" Rex asked, calling to check on the captain.

"I was doing okay, but I'm no longer captain, remember?" asked Hillary. "How are you doing? You sound like you're in an upbeat mood."

"Oh, I'm doing okay. Guess who called asking for my help?" asked Rex, laughing.

"No, don't tell me, you mean Eric Wilkson actually called you asking for help?" asked Hillary, feeling good there was a chance to get his job back.

"Yep, he called me and left a message because I was out on the deck," replied Rex. "He stated he is stumped on the kidnapping case of Frieda Schumacher with no leads or clues."

Hillary laughed. "So, he's stumped as what to do with no leads, is he? That is funny!" declared Hillary. "What are you going to do, help him?"

"No, I called the police station and left a message that I'm too busy on a case, and he said he didn't need my help, or Anne's."

"So, you're going to leave him to stew in his own mess? Rex Morgan, you're wicked!" replied Hillary, laughing. "I'm glad you never left me hanging like that. How is Anne doing? You two visiting each other's houses, I suppose?"

"Something like that, when I'm not busy with a case," replied Rex. "When I'm on a case, she goes to the art gallery, shops at the malls, goes to a play, and has lunch."

"The life of luxury!" moaned Hillary.

"Well, she lost all that money she schemed from the Militia's Militia, but she has her inheritance to live on," stated Rex. "Yeah, some people have all of the luck and others have none!"

"Oh, I don't know, I have a feeling Eric is going to louse up his job so bad they'll have to ask you to come back as Police Chief," replied Rex.

"That would make my day!" declared Hillary.

As time went on, it looked like Frieda Schumacher was gone, never to be seen or heard of again; a mark against Eric Wilkson on his first real case! *Is this the way it's going to be?* Eric wondered. *Being Police Chief isn't so easy. I made a big mistake in declaring the police could solve its own cases, or else they can't be solved! That was an arrogant statement I have to make right and live up to, or else admit my stupidity and need of help from time to time.*

Karl and Gertrud Schumacher came to Rex and asked if he would look into the disappearance of their daughter, and handed Rex a picture of Frieda. Anne, being there, was asked to sit in because she was an expert at disappearing and disguises. Rex stated he'd need Anne to be on the case as well. Karl and Gertrud understood. Anne listened to the conversation and watched the parents' expressions.

"Did you all get along well? She didn't have any hang-ups or moods?" asked Anne.

"Oh, she'd have a moody day occasionally, but nothing serious or worrisome," replied the mother.

"What would she do on days of moodiness? Go off by herself, or stay in her room?"

"She'd be sort of quiet all day. Otherwise, she was a happy person, full of life," replied Gertrud with a worried frown.

"Did she have any causes or ideals she strongly believed in?" Anne continued to quiz.

"Nothing I know of that would cause her to run off like this, if that's what you're wondering," declared the mother.

"Just what are you suggesting?" asked Karl, looking at Anne agitated at such an idea.

"Sometimes young people run off for some strong belief or cause to join up with the group of that cause." stated Anne. "I had to ask to clear that away for a reason. Well, that's cleared away then," replied Anne, taking note Karl got upset easily.

Rex noticed it too.

"The two of you are going to work on this together?" asked Karl.

"Yes. Anne comes up with ideas as a woman I might not think of, and she is good detecting if someone is in disguise or hiding something," replied Rex. "The housekeeper just up and called the police without consulting with you? What is her name?"

"Her name is Margaret Muller; we've known her for a long time, about eighteen years. Afterward, she was sorry about calling, but she thought she was doing the right thing. That's the first time she's done anything without consulting with us," stated Karl.

"How long has she been working for you?" asked Rex, wondering about the housekeeper.

"She has worked for us ten years; always on time and never complaining or slamming anybody, causes, or ideals," replied Karl.

"What about her family and friends? What are they like?"

"Her family and ours grew up pretty close to each other; nice, respectable people. Her friends are okay, as far as I know. She gets an occasional phone call from them, but I don't know them personally," stated Karl.

"I met one of her friends a while back. Vicky Tomean came to visit her on the terrace out back, stayed an hour," replied Gertrud.

"Does she talk about them, what they're like, what they do, or where they go?" continued Rex.

"She doesn't talk a lot about them; a little sometimes, but mostly her family."

"Her friends would be the ones I'd check out; they may be okay, but I suspect someone who knew you or your daughter might've had something to do with your daughter's disappearance," stated Rex. "Have you had any serious disagreements with anyone? A run-in with anyone? What do you for a living?"

"I own a construction company, 'Max's Construction'. I build homes, office buildings, warehouses, etc. I can't remember any serious arguments. As far as disagreements, yes," stated Karl.

The disagreements are something to consider. Someone might have taken the disagreements more serious than you thought," stated Rex. "Who did you have a disagreement with?"

Heinrich Hofmann of the Reynold Warehouse. e is always looking to undercut prices regardless of how low they are. He doesn't care if you sell yourself short, not as long he can make a steal," replied Karl.

"I would definitely check him out. Anybody else? Maybe some years back, someone was really upset?"

"A few years back, I outbid a competing company, an office building, Vincent Price, the owner has never gotten over it," admitted Karl.

"Well, this information will do as a start. Sometimes when people lose a bid they really wanted, or have a disagreement, they don't get over it, even though you passed it off," stated Rex.

"The police chief and the detective questioned the two clients, but they didn't get anything useful," replied Karl.

With this over for now, Anne went into the kitchen to fix coffee, asking Gertrud if she'd like to help with setting the on the table.

"Sure," Gertrud said and joined Anne in the kitchen.

"While Rex is doing his investigation, I could keep an eye out for your daughter. I have had experience in disappearing when I didn't want to be found, or I can find out if someone is with her," stated Anne. "We'll need to see her room to get a feel of what she's like, her tastes, and so on."

"Okay, you can come on over and see her room, the average young woman's taste," stated Gertrud. "I don't think she ran off on her own; I think someone kidnapped her."

Rex and Anne followed Karl and Gertrud to their house in to look at Frieda's room. Frieda's room had a nice, floral design pattern—red, pink, yellow, and purple—a nice layout. A picture of Frieda sat on a nightstand, and a picture of her with three friends in front of what looked like a library or college sat on the chest.

"These three friends of hers, do they stay in touch and live around here?" asked Anne.

"They live in a dorm at the college, Oakland University," Gertrud replied. "They get together and call occasionally. The Police Chief questioned them, but they had no knowledge of Frieda's disappearance. They call about twice a week to see if we've heard from her."

"Where did she hang out, and with whom?" Anne asked.

"There is a little village with a small café, Pierre's, she likes and went there occasionally, and she became friends with the owner, Pierre Girard. Frieda goes there sometimes with her three friends, Marianna, Nicole, and Margret. Sometimes Fritz, also a friend, will show up."

"Rex and I will need to get in touch with them soon as possible to see if they know anything. Sometimes people know something but don't think it's important. Rex will find her, I am sure of that!" stated Anne.

Gertrud gave Anne the phone number of the dorm where the three girls lived. Rex decided to check out Heinrich Hofmann and Vincent Price to see if they knew anything.

Reynold Warehouse was located on the outskirts of town on the main drag. On his way to the office, Heinrich was on the phone. Rex waited until he hung up and knocked on the door.

"Heinrich Hofmann, I am Rex Morgan, and I'd like to ask you a few questions concerning your business relationship with Karl Schumacher."

"Oh, we get along okay. He never gives me any breaks on prices or deals, but other than that, we're okay," stated Heinrich. "Why are you asking me about him? Who are you to question me?"

"I am a licensed investigator, and I'm investigating the disappearance of his daughter, Frieda," replied Rex.

"Well, the police and a detective have already questioned me, but I didn't have anything to do with that, nor do I know anything!" snapped Heinrich Hofmann.

"Are you sure you don't know anything?" inquired Rex. "It's better to say so now than in court under oath, rest assure of that!"

"I don't know anything, neither am I in any way involved!"

"Okay, we'll see. I may want to talk to you again later." assured Rex.

"You'll be talking to my lawyer if you do. I told the police I don't know anything, and now I'm telling you!" declared Heinrich. "You're not going to hang that on me!"

"I'm not trying to hang anything on you, but you are a person-of-interest in her disappearance."

"Well, I didn't do it, and I don't know anything about it! Before you make accusations, you had better have some hard evidence to back you up." declared Heinrich.

With that, Rex headed to to talk to Vincent Price. His secretary said he was on a job.

Rex, identifying himself, told her he needed to talk to him.

She said she'd have to contact him, but there was no answer on his cellphone.

"Well, I can talk to him now, or I can talk to him later, or he can talk in court!" declared Rex Morgan.

"I can keep trying to reach him. He must be away from his phone. Sometimes he leaves it in the truck when he's on a job," replied the secretary.

"I prefer to talk to him in person," stated Rex.

"I'll keep trying to reach him. What does this concern, if I may ask?"

"It is about the disappearance of Karl Schumacher's daughter, Frieda, and Vincent Price is a person-of-interest in her disappearance," replied Rex.

An hour later, Vincent called Rex. "Rex, I didn't have anything to do with the girl's disappearance, and I don't know anything about it. I have already told the police that. I'm a very busy man and don't have time to answer a bunch of questions when I already gave my answers." stated Vincent Price.

"You didn't take losing a bid to Karl Schumacher on a job very well, and my understanding is you haven't gotten over it! That makes you a person-of-interest in this case. You have motive!" declared Rex.

"Yes, that's true, but I'm not involved in any way, and I don't know anything! Far as that bid, Karl Schumacher underhandedly outbid me! That wasn't right and he knows it!" stated Vincent Price.

"I don't know the details of that, but you are a person-of-interest in Frieda Schumacher's disappearance," stated Rex.

"I was going to do anything; it wouldn't be against her but on him! She didn't have anything to do with what he did, so why grab her when he's to blame with what he did?"

"Well I may need to talk to you later," replied Rex.

"Only with my lawyer present!" declared Vincent Price.

"Do you know or have any idea who would grab her?" asked Rex.

"I figure it might be someone he pulled a dirty deal on or undermined!" suggested Vincent.

Rex later called Hillary to tell him Karl and Gertrud Schumacher came to him and Anne to locate their daughter.

"You're on the case of locating the daughter?" Hillary asked, laughing. "Wait until Eric finds this out. He'll feel like a fool! He'll freak!"

"Well, Karl and his wife asked Anne and I to find her, gave us a picture of her, and a fee of $120,000 to start," stated Rex.

Hillary laughed, feeling the chances of getting his job back greatly improved. "I hope you find her and bring her back home," declared Hillary, feeling Eric's time was short if this was the best he could do.

"Anne will be checking for Frieda in disguise, or if she's with someone." "So, both of you are in this together, you two belong together," replied Hillary.

"She lives in her house, but comes to visit. We'll be working on this together."

"Wait until Eric Wilkson hears about this; he'll be humiliated. He couldn't solve the case, so you're on it now! You two are professionals!" declared Hillary.

"I didn't ask for this case. Karl and Gerund came to Anne and me, giving us $120,000 to start," declared Rex. "I have two suspects so far, but I don't have anything on them yet."

"That doesn't surprise me, you and Anne are good at this!" declared Hillary. "Good luck. I hope you find her!"

"Thank you, I hope we do too," replied Rex, "for her sake and her parents' sake, as well."

Anne called the number of three friends, but got their voicemail. Anne left a message that she was trying to locate Frieda and needed to talk to them.

Three hours later, Nicole called Anne. "Anne, you trying to locate Frieda? Who are you, and why do you want to find her?" asked Nicole.

"Rex Morgan and I have been hired by Karl and Gertrud Schumacher to look for Frieda. We need to talk to you soon as possible."

"We don't really know anything about her disappearance," replied Nicole.

"You might know more than you think, sometimes that happens."

"Meet us at Pierre's then, but I don't think we can tell you anything more than we already told the police," stated Nicole.

"We haven't talked to the police yet, we're starting out fresh to pick up anything the police might have missed or overlooked," stated Anne.

"We'll tell you what we know, such as it is, we miss Frieda. We hung out together occasionally when we weren't in class, at the library, or studying, or here at the café," stated Nicole.

At the café, Rex and Anne talked to the three girls, Marina, Nicole, and Margret meeting at the café. Sometimes they had a fruit drink, sometimes with a snack, talked and joked. Sometimes Fritz would show up to join in; he is a classmate at the college."

"We need to get in touch with Fritz," stated Rex. "Did you ever notice anyone hanging around, acting a bit suspicious in any way?"

"There was a finicky guy, cook in the back; he sometimes watched us while he cleaned tables inside," added Marina.

"Ah, he is gone now; he liked girls, but was shy around us. He was harmless though, I'm sure," replied Margret. "We never said anything to the police because we figured he was harmless."

"You never know, he could be the one we're looking for. When did he leave?" asked Rex.

"About four months ago," said Marina. "You think he could be the one?"

"Sounds like he could be a person-of-interest. The ones you think are innocent can be the very one who would do the crime. I need a description of this guy," declared Rex.

"He was about 5'8", weighed about 180 lbs., brown, shortcut hair, with a slight limp on the right side," stated Marina.

With that, Rex went in the café to talk to Pierre to see what he knew about the cook, and if Pierre gave the same description as Marina.

"Ron Belmore was a good cook and worker, always on time, never bothered anybody, but always courteous to the customers," stated Pierre.

"Did he seem a bit funny to you as the girls out there suggested? A bit shy?" quizzed Rex.

"He was shy, especially around those girls. He would've liked to talk to them, but he was just too shy."

"I need his address and phone number," requested Rex.

"I have his address, but I think he has moved. I've called him as to why he hasn't shown up for work, but there was no answer," declared Pierre.

"Well, I still need his address," stated Rex.

Pierre went to his employee file and wrote down Ron Belmore's address, giving it to Rex.

"I need a description of him too."

Pierre gave a description of Ron, about 5'8", about 180 lbs., brown hair shorthair, and a slight limp on the right side.

Rex and Anne drove to Ron's address at a boarding house on the lower eastside of Berkley, a shabby run-down building. Both Rex and Anne go to the manager's apartment to talk to him.

A middle-aged, long haired, and bearded man came to the door in baggy, ripped jeans.

"Yeah, what ya' want?" he asked with a slight slang. "You're not here for an apartment, I can see that!"

"You the manager of this boarding house?" asked Rex.

"Yeah, what of it? What ya' want?" he asked again.

"Does Ron Belmore live here?"

"Who are you, the police?"

"I am Rex Morgan, a licensed investigator, and this is Anne Towers, my assistant. We are looking for Ron Belmore and we want to know if he lives here?" Rex asked the manager.

"What has he done?" the manager asked.

"He is a person-of-interest in an investigation. Now, are you going to answer my question?" declared Rex.

"An investigation into what?"

"Just answer the question!" demanded Rex. "Is he related to you? Are you trying to hinder an investigation?"

"No, he is not related to me. He is behind, he stiffed me on rent!" replied the manager. "He just up and moved without saying a word!"

Rex and Anne looked around unimpressed with a sour expression.

"Oh, I know, it's not near as nice as where you more than likely live, but with the bums who live here, why bother?" declared the manager. "I know it's not the most glorious place to live. but it's what they can afford and willing to pay! I don't have a hefty income like you two probably do. I knew when you came here you weren't interested in an apartment. It's not as nice!"

"Can we see his apartment?" asked Rex, ignoring the slurred comments.

"I threw everything out after he skipped out. There's nothing in there now!"

"Did he give any reference as to where he used to live?" asked Anne.

"No, he said he didn't have any, but I didn't believe him. I figured he stiffed them as well as me!" replied the manager angrily.

"Can we see his apartment anyway?"

"You won't find anything but an empty apartment," declared the manager, leading the way up the narrow, creaky stairs, in need of repair, to the side of the boarding house, litter scattered about, the yard a mess, no grass. Sure enough, the apartment was totally empty except the greasy strove and dingy looking refrigerator. The windows smeared, and the apartment needed to be aired out, a bit stuffy, and a foul odor.

Rex and Anne looked around in each room making sure they didn't touch anything, but saw nothing except in a corner a small wad of paper. Rex immediately went over and picked it up, unfolding it. Rex showed it to Anne.

"It's Frieda's address!" Anne exclaimed.

"You found something?" the manager asked, surprised.

"The address of a person-of-interest," replied Rex.

With that, they went back downstairs. "We need a description of Ron Belmore," declared Rex.

"He's about 5'8", weighs about 170-180 lbs., brown, cut hair, and has a slight limp on the right side," stated the manager. "If you find him, he owes two months' rent, and I want it!"

"Did anybody come to see him?" asked Rex.

"I don't know, I don't pay much attention as long as they don't have any wild parties and tear up the place," replied the manager.

"You know you're supposed to keep this place up to safety code and standards; this place is a safety hazard; a building inspector would write you up for this place being in such hazardous condition. If someone fell and hurt themselves, they could sue you for a bundle!" declared Rex.

"They wouldn't get anything from me because I don't have anything, and I don't own this dump. I just manage and collect the rent for the owner," replied the manager.

"You need to pass word to him to fix this place up before the building inspector shuts it down! The stairs on the side are too risky, it shakes when you climb the steps, and the stairs are too narrow, there is a smell of mildew and dampness in the apartment, the floors squeak when you walk, and need refinishing. There isn't enough light in the rooms, ventilation is bad, a crack or two in the walls and ceiling. The windows aren't tight enough, a breeze seeping in, need replacing," replied Rex.

"Is that it?" asked the manager sourly.

"I would think that'd be enough what I saw glancing around. A building inspector would be a lot more demanding," replied Rex.

"I tell him that and he'd probably shut it down! Then I'd be out of a job! Then what would I do?"

"Well, I'm just warning you in case a building inspector comes around. If he does, you'll be out of a job anyway."

"We need to locate this Ron Balmoral," Rex told Anne out of ear-range of the manager on the way back to the car.

The manager, dispirited, watched Rex and Anne leave.

"How do we locate him before he finds out we're looking for him?" asked Anne. "If he gets wind of our plans, he'll more than likely make a run for it!"

"We'll go to the courthouse to look up his birthplace and if he has any living relatives. If we locate his relatives, we'll stake out their house to see if we see him, and if he doesn't show, then we'll question the relatives," stated Rex. "We'll also check if he associated with any felons or suspects at the police station."

"And have a confrontation with Eric Wilkson asking a thousand questions?" asked Anne.

"I could call a clerk and have him check Ron's record and see if he associated with any suspicious characters. Hillary could have him check for me too."

"I like that idea better. Eric may not wonder about Hillary, maybe."

"Oh, Eric doesn't bother me. I'm on a case," replied Rex.

At the courthouse, Rex and Anne requested Ron Belmore's birth record and showed his investigator's license to the clerk in charge of births and deaths. The clerk recorded Rex's and Anne's names, then retrieves the birth record. Rex wrote down the date of Ron Belmore's birth, birthplace, and the hospital in Charleston, West Virginia.

Rex called Hillary to have him see if Ron Belmore had associated with any felons.

"I can have Roni Stogy run a check on him; he works in the records department," replied Hillary, glad to be of use and on good terms with Rex again.

"I would appreciate it," replied Rex.

Sure enough, Ronald (Ron) Belmore had been seen with a well-known felon and person-of-interest, Loui Binoche, in unsolved breaking and entering and felony murder. Charged, but never convicted, it was suspected he had connections in getting off, but somebody paid for his high-priced lawyer. Who else could afford such an expensive lawyer? He might have been a snitch for the FBI, Justice Department, or he knew something that needed to be kept quiet.

"Is there an address for Loui Binoche?" asked Rex.

"Yes, there is, if you want to go there, but I wouldn't take Anne, not if you care for her," cautioned Hillary. "Loui Binoche stays in an upstairs apartment above Spic's Grill at 6085 Balta Street, a lower class, ruff neighborhood," stated Hillary nervously. "That neighborhood is dangerous! People have disappeared there and don't talk! It's a code of silence with them, it's law! That neighborhood reeks with violence and death!"

"I'll talk to her about it. We could meet up later," replied Rex, considering Hillary warning.

"That would be a very wise decision." replied Hillary. "Just thinking about that place makes me nervous. I haven't been there, but I've certainly heard plenty about it."

"Is there a description of Loui Binoche?"

Hillary looked at Rex, shaking his head. "He's 5'10", 220 pounds, dirty blonde hair, has a droopy left eye, and he's a mean guy to mess with. He doesn't like being questioned and he has a bad temper." replied Hillary, nervously. If you go there, good luck. Look for your picture in the newspaper."

"Thank you, Hillary. That was a big help!" replied Rex, thinking of what Hillary said.

"I just hope to see you again, alive!"

"Hillary says this apartment above Spic's Grill being on Balta Street is in a low class, rough neighborhood, and it's dangerous. Hillary says Loui is a mean guy to mess with who doesn't like being questioned, and he has a bad temper. Maybe you shouldn't go there with me, but we could meet later," stated Rex. "He was really nervous talking about it. He said if I go, he wished me luck, but he'll be looking for my picture in the newspaper."

"People in that neighborhood avoid talking to strangers, people don't like," stated Anne. "You don't get nosey, go prowling around, and don't go into isolated places. The place is dingy with litter scattered everywhere and people hanging around in threes and fours glaring at you. From what I've heard, it's like a sewer in there. If the police ever show up, the people go into hiding."

"How do you know that? Have you been there?" asked Rex surprised. "Sounds like no place for you to be."

"Yes, I have been there, but I was an outsider to them, and they were downright rude and cold. I didn't stay there for long. I kept moving," replied Anne. "I'll go with you, but I'm not leaving you alone in isolated places. No snooping around or asking too many questions. You could catch a disease in there, and, if you're not careful, you could catch death."

"I hear you there!" replied Rex. "We need to talk to this Loui Binoche if we find him."

"I doubt you'll find him or he'll talk to you. If you do find him, don't push him to talk. You could get killed that way."

"I'm on them if we can find them," Rex told Anne, heading for home, trying to have hope. "First, we try to find Loui Binoche to talk to him, and then find Ron Belmore to talk to him."

"I figure we'll have more luck finding Ron Belmore than Loui Binoche and it would be safer, but we need to let Karl and Gertrud know we're looking for Loui and Ron for now," reminded Anne.

"Oh yeah, we don't want to get their hopes up just yet."

"Good, we're glad you're getting somewhere, which is more than the police chief and detective were able to do!" stated Karl.

"We can't promise anything as far as these two guys, and we've yet to find them, but they are persons-of-interest for now," stated Rex.

"Thank you for calling us and letting us know something," replied Karl.

Rex and Anne called Hillary, and then headed for Spic's Grill to look for Loui, and, by luck, question him. Hillary, hearing Rex and Anne were still looking for Loui, became extremely nervous, telling Rex, "It's been nice knowing you, good lord."

The neighborhood was grimy, litter scattered everywhere, streets not well-lit, one street light busted, and people stood around in threes and fours watching and glaring at Rex and Anne as they drove down Balta Street, hardly any cars on the streets. Rex and Anne were nervous being there.

Spotting Spic's Grill, Rex and Anne went in to look for Loui. Inside, the customers, street people mostly, glared at Rex and Anne with cold, hardened eyes and expressions, watching like buzzards. Rex and Anne took a table close to the door, keeping an eye on their car, and observed the gawking onlookers sitting around, one guy with a far-away look, expressionless.

A middle-aged, stringy-haired guy in filthy, ragged clothes staggered over and asked, "Just who are you looking for? What do you want?"

"We're looking for Loui Binoche. Have you seen him or know where he is?" asked Rex.

"Don't know him," the guy replied. "I wouldn't say even if I did know him. We don't rat on each other! You could get killed for that!"

"We just want to talk to him, that is all."

"I still don't know him, and I wouldn't say even I did! Who is he to you?"

"We want to know if he has seen Ron Belmore or talked to him," stated Rex. "That is all we want."

"I don't know Loui Binoche, but this is a really bad neighborhood to be in, very bad for your health!" stated the guy, angrily. "What is Ron Belmore to you? Are you related?"

"No, we're not related, but we feel Loui or Ron Belmore might know someone we're looking for," stated Rex.

"There's a lot of people you're looking for. You the police or something?" the guy continued quizzing.

"No, we are not the police. I am a private investigator, and she is my assistant," replied Rex. "We're looking for a girl who was kidnapped."

"I don't know either one of them, but no one rats on each other here if they want to live!"

"Let's go to the upstairs apartments and see if Loui Binoche is there," suggested Rex to Anne.

"I wouldn't do that; strangers and outsiders aren't welcomed in these apartment buildings or even on the streets in this neighborhood! You could get seriously hurt or killed roaming around in these apartments and the streets, and no one would say a word or do anything. You could disappear quickly!" he exclaimed in a hateful tone, glaring at Rex and Anne.

"Who are you, then?"

"I am nobody to you!"

With that, he staggered back to the bar talking low to the bartender and two other street men, who glared at Rex and Anne. After about five minutes, one hazard-looking guy with a hopeless look staggered out the door. Rex and Anne sat for thirty minutes, waiting to see if Loui Binoche came in, but he never showed. The on-lookers continued to sit staring at Rex and Anne.

"It looks like Loui isn't going to show. That guy who staggered out probably told Loui two people are looking for him," stated Anne. "We might as well leave, he's not going to show as long as we're here. It'd not be good to still be here when the sun sets." Anne was extremely nervous.

"No, I don't feel it would be good either. We better leave now," stated Rex. "We need to go home to pack and leave for West Virginia, locate, and stake out Ron's parents to keep a watch on their house."

Hillary was relieved to hear Rex and Anne made it back from that rough neighborhood; he didn't figure Rex and Anne would find Loui Binoche, not in that neighborhood.

Anne, with her luggage, returned to Rex's house to find he fixed a meal before they start on the trip. On the counter were a few snacks and pop to munch on the road. Rex's camera and equipment were also on the counter in case he saw Ron by himself or with his family doing something questionable.

With the luggage all packed and loaded in the trunk of Rex's car, and the camera and equipment in the backseat, the snacks upfront, Rex and Anne lockup their houses and start off to Craigsville, West Virginia to stake out Ron Belmore's family. Rex and Anne traded off driving to give each other a chance to relax and rest; stopping along the way for a meal and making pitstops. Halfway to Craigsville, they stopped at a motel for the night. The next morning, they had breakfast and started out again.

Arriving in Craigsville, they located a Best Western Hotel, had dinner, and relaxed. Obtaining a map of the local area, they found the Belmore family's street. Bill and Martha Belmore, the parents living on Sleigh Road, ran into Cherry Run Road, and then Route 20.

The uncle and Aunt Mary Lou Belmore lived on Cherry Run, which connected to Cherry Run Road, a short piece from Sleigh Road. Rex and Anne, tired from the trip, decided to relax and try to find Ron early the next morning. The small-town people were interesting to watch and listen. There were one or two men in bib overalls and straw hats; an amusing sight for Anne. The general feeling was this is (Rue' folks in a small southern town. There was a lot of "You'll come, ja hear?" There were also a lot of "Y'all take care, do hear?" with a southern drawl. It was all Anne could do to keep from laughing.

Rex glanced at Anne, who held herself to keep from laughing .

"I'm glad I came along; this is an experience I'm enjoying," declared Anne, about to split-a-gut.

"I can tell. I figured you would, sort of like another world compared to what we're used to," replied Rex with a smile. "These are just plain ol' southern folks."

"So, I see," replied Anne, grinning. "You think they might have beauty salons, fashion malls, and boutiques around here?" Anne asked, jokingly.

"I seriously doubt it," replied Rex, laughing and shaking his head. "You're high maintenance for them."

"Boo-hoo," replied Anne, laughing with Rex, who still shook his head.

"We'd like some breakfast menus, please," Rex told the waiter the next morning in a restaurant.

"Oh, okay," the waiter said, smiling and taking the lunch menus. He retrieved the breakfast menus.

"To get breakfast, you must get up early, at dawn, and some do," Rex told Anne. "The farmers get up at sunrise to start their day and the stores accommodate the farmers. They feel sleeping in is wasting a good part of the day."

While having breakfast, Rex and Anne checked the local map to locate Cherry Run and Sleigh Roads. They slowly drove by the uncle and aunt's house, and then the parents' house. Rex and Anne saw the uncle and aunt sitting on the front porch, but the parents must've been inside their house, or not at home. Rex and Anne parked a block and half away and staked out the parents' house. While sitting almost all morning and nobody showed, Rex decided to swing by the uncle and aunt's again, but they either went inside or left; their door was closed. After a couple of hours, they pulled up in their driveway.

"Let's talk to them and see if they know where Ron is," suggested Anne.

"We might as well; it's apparent he isn't around here, unless he's living somewhere in town," replied Rex. "See if they've heard from him or know where he is."

The uncle and aunt, on seeing Rex and Anne coming to talk to them, stopped and watched curiously as Rex and Anne approached.

"Hi, I am Rex Morgan, and this is Anne Towers. We were wondering if you have seen or talked to your nephew, Ron Belmore."

"How do you know Ron, and how do you know us?" asked the uncle. "Who are you?"

"I am an investigator and Anne is my assistant. We know he knew Frieda Schumacher and Ron had her address. Frieda has disappeared or run off, and her parents are worried sick. We would like to talk to Ron to see if he knows where Frieda could have gone and when he last talked to her," stated Rex.

"I talked to him a couple days ago; he got behind on his rent, so he skipped his apartment. He said the manager always wants it on the first of the month and not to be late, but the place is a dump!" stated the uncle.

"He's a good boy. Is he in any kind of trouble?" asked the aunt, concerned.

"No, he's not in kind of trouble that we know. We just want to talk to him about Frieda," replied Rex. "We saw the apartment and it is a dump alright, but the manager said Ron was two months behind on his rent. If the manager wants the rent on the first of the month, how could he be behind two months?"

"Oh, the manager was trying to get more money than Ron owes. He's a chiseler!" declared the uncle. "Are you with the police?"

"No, we are not with the police," replied Anne. "We're just trying to find Frieda Schumacher for her parents, who are worried sick as to her whereabouts."

"You think our nephew has anything to do with her disappearance?" asked the uncle, aggravated at Rex and Anne for even suggesting that.

"We aren't saying he had anything to do with it, but he might know if she left on her own or with somebody suspicious. We need to know when he talked to her last. He might know something, anything that could help us find Frieda."

"He never mentioned her to us. If he calls again, we could have him contact you," suggested the uncle.

With that, Rex gave them the phone number, name of the hotel, and room number he and Anne were staying.

Rex and Anne swung back by the parents' house and, seeing them sitting on the front porch, decided to stop and ask if they'd talked to, or seen, Ron.

"I am Rex Morgan, and she is Anne Towers. We are looking for your son, Ron Belmore, to talk to him about Frieda Schumacher."

"We talked to him a couple of days ago when he dropped by. Is he involved in something?" asked the father.

"No, not that we know, we just want to ask if he has seen or talked to Frieda Schumacher recently. She has been missing for a while now, and the parents are worried. We're trying to locate anybody who might have seen or talked to her. He had her address in his apartment," stated Rex. "We have seen the apartment, and it is a dump alright. I wouldn't stay there for anything! The manager looked at home in it though," stated Rex with a slight grin. "The uncle said the manager charges on the first of the month, but the manager told us Ron was behind two months on his rent."

"I wouldn't stay there either!" declared Anne.

"The rent was way too high considering the condition it was in. If Ron comes by or calls, we could have him contact," stated the mother.

Rex gave her the phone number, name of the hotel, and room number where he and Anne were staying.

"You think he'll contact us?" asked Anne as they returned to the car.

"If he has nothing to hide, he might. Whether he knows where she is, is anybody's guess," replied Rex. "We can continue to stake out the parents' and the uncle and aunt's house, or wait to see if he comes by."

"He may check us out first if he's around here," stated Anne.

"I don't mind that. I feel he might be around here somewhere, but his parents, uncle, and aunt want to check with him first before they reveal his whereabouts," replied Rex thoughtfully.

"Can't blame them for that, they're family."

"True. I have seen families who are related, but distant, and I have seen families who are related and stick together through thick and thin," stated Rex.

"So have I," stated Anne.

Rex wondered how things were back at home and called Hillary to have him check on their houses.

"I've kept a check on both your houses and they are fine. Eric Wilkson has heard about you two working on Frieda's disappearance and he is super mad you are moving forward on the case when he ran into a dead-end," stated Hillary laughing.

"How did he find out?" asked Rex amused.

"Oh, some clerk over at the courthouse told him that case of Frieda Schumacher missing, you two are working on it at Karl and Gertrud Schumacher's request, and someone at the police station told him as well. Eric wonders how you found out so much in such a brief time.

He says if you have any information, you're supposed to turn it over to the police," declared Hillary, amused.

"We don't have anything definite to report. All we have is a person-of-interest, if we can find him, but we don't have anything on him yet, just an curious hunch. Eric just wants to hinder Anne and me from solving the case, or else help him solve it himself when he couldn't, and we're making him look bad," stated Rex. "Eric doesn't like to be shown up, especially after making the statement he will solve his own cases!"

Anne, who was close by, overheard Rex and wondered what was up listening intently.

"Oh, you're making him look bad, alright. Cheryl Nickels, Wayne Milton, Milton Bradley, and Larry Flippant have heard about how you two are moving forward on this case from the courthouse. It's leaked out to Jan Roberts and Harold Jacobs you two are on this case, but that is all they know. They got wind of it by eavesdropping."

"Someone at the courthouse is talking, and at the police station as well," repliedRex.

"How did you hear about it? Did Eric tell you?"

"Alright, good going, Hillary!" exclaimed Rex. "Maybe you'll get back in there after he has showed himself up. I was willing to help you on your cases. And if you do get back in, I'll help you again, if I can. It didn't matter that you got the credit, I was glad to be able to help because of our friendship."

"I appreciated it and I still do," replied Hillary. "I have been keeping an eye on both of your houses, but I haven't seen any suspicious activity as of yet. So, this Ron Belmore is a possible suspect, you think?"

"Thank you for watching our houses. We really appreciate it. As for now, Ron Belmore is just a person-of-interest until we have more information about him and what he knows," stated Rex. "We haven't located him yet, but I feel it's just a matter of time. I suspect when we get to Berkley, Jan Roberts and Harold Jacobs will be waiting to interview us on the case."

"They've already heard you and Anne are on the case, but haven't made any statement yet. I think they're waiting for you all to get back," stated Hillary.

"What's up in Berkley?" asked Anne after Rex had hung up.

"Oh, Eric Wilkson has found out that we're working on this case and he is mad that we're moving forward on it when he got nowhere on it," replied Rex grinning. Anne laughs hearing that.

"Hillary heard Jan Roberts and Harold Jacobs had gotten wind we're working on this case, but were waiting for us to come back to interview us. Hillary says Eric feels if we come up with any information, we're supposed to turn it over to the police so they can continue their investigation," stated Rex.

"So, he'll look good, huh? Let him solve it on his own, that's what he wanted," stated Anne.

"Yes, but we're making him look bad. Cheryl Nickels, Wayne Milton, Milton Bradley, and Larry Flippant have heard about us moving forward on this case from the courthouse and the police station," stated Rex.

"I guess Eric is really embarrassed then. Teach him not to be so arrogant!" declared Anne angrily with a smirk.

"I wonder where Ron Belmore is?" pondered Rex aloud.

"Just keep up the stakeout is all I can think of," replied Anne. "Going into that neighborhood on Balta Street was really risky; people disappear in neighborhoods like that and no one says or does anything! Nobody talks in those neighborhoods! We're lucky we got out alive! It wouldn't be good to be in there after dark, I hope we don't have to go back there, or any neighborhoods like that."

"Yeah, we were lucky alright. I don't how people survive in neighborhoods like that, or how they end up there," replied Rex.

"Drugs and alcohol, or being on the run from the law drives them there," stated Anne. "Seldom does anyone walk away from there; you could catch a disease or die."

"Are you speaking from experience?" asked Rex.

"I have rubbed shoulders with people from places like that; they have a code they live by and for them it is law."

"I imagine you have had some life experiences in hiding. I hope I never have to experience something like that." stated Rex.

"It's an experience that slays with you, makes you thankful for what you have." declared Anne murkily.

"Yeah, I guess it does." replied Rex solemnly.

Ron Belmore came up the sidewalk to his parents' house and knocked on the door. Rex and Anne saw him, quickly got out of the car, and crossed the street just as Ron was let in the house. Rex knocked on the door and the father answered.

"Yes?"

"We just saw your son come in your house. We need to talk to him," stated Rex.

"Just a minute," the father replied.

Ron came to the door aggravated, "Yes? Who are you and what do you want?"

"I am Rex Morgan, a private investigator, and she is Anne Towers, my assistant. We need to talk to you about Frieda Schumacher; we need to know where she is. Her parents are frantic," stated Rex.

"I don't know where she is. I liked her and talked to her occasionally, but that was it," replied Ron.

"You don't know where she went?" asked Rex sternly.

"No, I don't know. I suppose she went somewhere with her friends; they always seemed so close. It was like I wasn't in the group, that Fritz liked her a lot," declared Ron.

"Really?" asked Anne.

"Yeah, he did. he was crazy about her. I didn't stand a chance with him around and I think he didn't like me looking at her," replied Ron.

"Was he jealous of her talking or looking at other guys?" asked Anne.

"Oh yeah, he didn't like it at all!" declared Ron. "The girlfriends knew it, I think."

"They didn't say anything about Fritz being jealous. Did they date?" asked Anne.

"I don't know, I stayed busy working. Pierre didn't like talking on his time. I didn't have a chance to talk to the girls while working or with Fritz around," stated Ron.

"Maybe we need to take another look at Fritz then. Do you know his last name?" asked Rex.

"I only knew him as Fitz."

"We have been trying to find you for a number of days. We found your old apartment, but you skipped out without paying your rent, not that I can blame you! Where have you been?" asked Rex.

"Moving around, staying with friends, staying in a shelter," replied Ron.

"We need to confirm that. You haven't been hiding Frieda or keeping her somewhere?" asked Anne.

"No, I told you I haven't seen her or know where she is!"

"We need to confirm where you've been staying; addresses and names," stated Rex.

Ron wrote down the address of a friend he had stayed with and the name and address of the shelter, "Friends' Shelter".

"Oh, there is one more thing we need to clear up," stated Rex. "We've learned that you associated with Loui Binoche and we've tried to locate him to question him as well. Following the lead led us to Balta Street in a real rough neighborhood. You wouldn't know where he is, would you?"

"I stopped associating with him because is bad news! You can be glad you didn't find him; he wouldn't take you finding him well. People who cross or question him aren't around very long. I got away from him. Why would you want to contact him?" asked Ron.

"We thought he might know where you were, but we couldn't find him and the guy we talked to warned us not to go roaming around in the apartment buildings," replied Rex.

"He was right; you don't go roaming around in that neighborhood, or any neighborhood like that! People disappear and nobody does or says anything! They have a code of silence, and they live by it too!" exclaimed Ron. "I've never been there, but I've met people from there. They have emotional scars from being there. You're lucky you got out of there alive!"

Rex and Anne drove to the residential area close to town, locating the address Ron gave them, the saw a young man playing with a small dog in the yard.

"Hi, I am Rex Morgan. I am a licensed investigator and she is Anne Towers, my assistant. We need know if Ron Belmore stayed with you and for how long," stated Rex.

"Why do you need to know that? Are you cops? Did Ron do something wrong?"

"No, we're not cops. We are investigating Ron's acquaintances with a missing person." "Ron stayed here the last five nights. He isn't in some kind of trouble, is he?"

"We don't think so, but we have to confirm where he has been," replied Rex.

With that cleared, Rex and Anne drove to the shelter to confirm Ron's stay there. He had been there for a week. That cleared Ron Belmore of any wrongdoing, and returned suspicion to the three girls and Fritz.

Rex and Anne went back to the hotel to pack and return to Berkley and locate Fritz and question him, as well as the girls. Rex decided to call Karl Schumacher to let him know how things were going.

"Karl, this is Rex. We have finished tracking here. We found the person-of-interest here, but he is clear. He directed us back to a certain person, so we're coming back to locate and talk to this person."

"So, you're getting close to solving this kidnapping?"

"Well, I can't say until we talk to this person, but we're weeding through the people surrounding your daughter, one-by-one," replied Rex.

"At least you're making headway."

"We'll keep in touch."

With Karl and Gertrud being kept up to date, Rex called Hillary to see if anything new was happening. "How are things going?" inquired Rex.

"Oh, Jan Roberts and Harold Jacobs know for sure now you and Anne are working on the Frieda Schumacher kidnapping case, and they are waiting to interview you both. They came to ask me if I had heard from you," replied Hillary.

"What did you tell them?"

"I told them you were tracking a suspect, but you didn't have anything solid yet, and it is still up in the air as to who the culprit could be," stated Hillary.

"Well, we found that person and he's clean, but he directed us to a better suspect. We're going back there to talk to him," stated Rex.

"Someone around here?" asked Hillary excited.

"According to this person we talked to, yes. This person is a much better a suspect."

"Wow, things are getting interesting!" exclaimed Hillary. "Oh, I drove to both your houses and everything seems intact."

"Good."

"If you bring the guilty party to justice, Eric will never recover from that; you've made him look like a third-rate amateur, and he knows it!" stated Hillary. "Cheryl Nickels, Wayne Milton, Milton Bradley, and Larry Flippant are looking to you and Anne to solve this kidnapping."

"Jan Roberts and Harold Jacobs know we're working on the kidnapping case and Cheryl Nickels, Wayne Milton, Milton Bradley, and Larry Flippant feel you and I will bring the kidnapper to justice. Jan and Harold are waiting to interview us," declares Rex to Anne.

Pulling into the driveway, Hillary waited anxiously. He helped carry in the luggage up to Rex's house. Rex and Anne told him about tracking down Loui Binoche and ending up on Balta Street in a rough neighborhood a street light out, people standing around on the street glaring at them, and going into the grill/bar to look for Loui Binoche. They told Hillary about the rough-looking guy coming over to them to see what they were doing there and who they were looking for. They told Hillary they mentioned going to the upstairs apartments, but the guy said, "No!"

"The guy said strangers aren't welcomed in the apartment buildings, much less that neighborhood. He said people there don't rat on each other," stated Anne. "People disappear in neighborhoods like that."

"What were you doing in that neighborhood? You could've been killed and nobody would've known!" exclaimed Hillary nervously. "You actually went in the bar/grill?"

Rex said, "Yes."

Hillary nervously shook his head.

"Yes, we could've been killed, but that was where our lead on Loui Binoche took us, only we didn't find him," replied Rex. "There was one guy who staggered out the door. We think he went and told Loui we were looking for him, but he never showed."

"You're lucky to be alive!" exclaimed Hillary. "I'm glad I'm not in your line of work!"

"When you're investigating, you go where your lead takes you," stated Rex, smiling.

"However, we felt it best to leave before sunset, so we left."

"Yeah, good thing you did! You follow your leads if you don't end up dead!" replied Hillary, nervous thinking about the neighborhood.

"How about a good ol' cookout? I'm ready for one!" declared Anne.

Rex, Anne, and Hillary went out on the deck for the cookout and fire up the grill. Rex got the grill started as Anne told Hillary about their stay in Craigsville, West Virginia,. Hillary grinned and said it sounded like the good ol' days down there; they hadn't caught up with modern times yet. The doorbell rang.

"I wonder who that could be?" Rex said, going to the front door.

It was Jan Roberts and Harold Jacobs and the cameramen for an interview.

"We're all out on the deck having a cookout," Rex told them. "You'll have to come out there."

They follow Rex out on the deck.

Wait until Eric sees this on TV, Rex thought with a grin.

"Well, I guess we better put more steaks and pork chops on the grill," stated Anne.

"Hello, Hillary. Now we know where to find you," declared Jan Roberts, smiling.

On the deck, the cameras turned on as Rex and Anne discussed their investigation, only the highlights and the chilling experience on Balta Street. Jan and Harold listened intently while the cameramen recorded.

"Well, you all have had quite an experience then! Wow! I don't know if I'd follow a lead into a neighborhood like that; you could've been killed!" exclaimed Jan.

Harold shook his head. The cameramen were astounded.

"Oh, people disappear in neighborhoods like that, we were lucky," admitted Anne.

"Lucky, yeah, I'll say you were!" exclaimed Jan.

Harold nodded in agreement.

"You want to be an investigator?" Rex teased.

"No, don't think so!" Jan and Harold replied in unison. "Not at the risk of my life!" declared Jan.

With the pork chops and steaks done, plus the salads, beans, and potato salad, everybody dug in. Jan and Harold commented on the beauty of Rex's deck and backyard.

"My house is next door." Anne pointed to her house.

"Some people have it made," grumbled Harold with Jan.

The cameramen and Hillary looked on enviously as Rex and Anne smiled.

"Taking on cases pays for this home, "replied Rex.

"I had an inheritance from my father," stated Anne.

"The blessings of being well off!" declared Harold.

The next day, Rex and Anne thought of locating Fritz to question him.

"You know, it might be good to stake out the girls as well as Fritz; all of them might be involved," stated Anne.

"You think so?" asked Rex, considering the girls didn't say anything about Fritz being jealous, but Ron Belmore felt the girls knew. If they did, why didn't they say something? To protect Fritz? That put things in a different light, the girls with Fritz? They could be charged with kidnapping, as well Fritz, or accessory, depending on how involved they were. Well, the investigation wasn't over yet!

"The only way I know to stake out the girls and Fritz is to watch Pierre's Café wait, and then follow them to wherever they live and go," stated Rex.

"That would work," replied Anne.

Rex and Anne put on their disguises and headed to Pierre's, parking a couple blocks away.

Later that afternoon, Marina, Nicole, and Margret showed up, order their fruit drinks, and sat out on the patio of the café, laughing and talking. An hour later, Fritz showed up flirting with the girls as usual for an hour. Getting up, they walked in the direction away from their college dorm to a middle-income house in an urban neighborhood.

"Maybe this is where Fritz lives, or his folks," said Rex.

"Maybe," said Anne.

Rex and Anne sat a block away and watched as the girls and Fritz entered the house, Fritz unlocking the door.

"You want to sneak up and peek in the windows?" asked Rex.

"If we don't get caught," replied Anne.

They both casually walked up to Fritz's house and snuck around, peeking in the windows, seeing furniture but not the girls or Fritz. Maybe they were in the basement, but the basement windows were covered.

Rex and Anne met back on the sidewalk to decide what to do. To get inside, they would need a signed search warrant by a judge, and getting that would require probable cause. That would bring in Eric Wilkson, putting him in charge, he'd love that!

"We could wait until they come out and then question them," stated Rex, "but that would put them on guard knowing we suspect them."

"If they'd talk to us; officially, we can't make them talk," replied Anne.

"If they don't talk, then we'll know they have something to hide or some questionable reason to stay hushed," stated Rex. "That would really put the spotlight on them, which would give me reason to call Eric for sure."

"Yeah, and they wouldn't want that, but Erie would seek the credit for solving the case." replied Anne. "They are suspects, but we have nothing but our suspicions for now."

A couple of hours later, the girls and Fritz came walking out of the house to be met by a girl in pigtails in a white cotton blouse and short skirt. Rex, looking like an older man, maybe the grandfather.

"Well, hello, girls. Hi, Fritz!" said Anne, smiling, Rex at her side.

"Do we know you?" asked Marina.

"Sure you do. I'm Anne Towers," Anne said, removing her makeup.

"I am Rex Morgan. You all know us. We asked you about Frieda Schumacher, remember?"

"We told you everything we know," replied Margret.

"Not entirely! We found out Fritz is jealous if Frieda interacts with any boys other than him." stated Anne.

"That's out of line. Whoever told you that is lying big time," snared Fritz angrily.

"They sounded like they knew what they were talking about, and said you three girls knew he is jealous of Frieda!" stated Anne.

"That is a lie! We don't know or believe it," stormed Nicole. "Fritz isn't the jealous type!"

"Well, the person we talked to was sure of what he said" stated Rex.

"Who is this person?" stormed Fritz.

"Ron Belmore."

"Oh, you found him, and he said that about me?" asked Fritz surprised.

"Yes, and he was in saying it," stated Rex. "Do you live in that house?"

"Yes, I live there; it was a rental house belonging to my parents, but they let me live there now," stated Fritz.

"Frieda wouldn't happen to be in there, would she?" asked Anne curiously.

"Why would she be in there?"

"We strongly feel someone is holding her against her will," declared Anne as Rex watched Fritz's expression, as well as the girls.

The girls were surprised Anne would ask such a question.

"You think I'm holding Frieda in my house?" asked Fritz aggravated.

"We don't think she ran away.," stated Rex.

"Well, it's not me!" bellowed Fritz.

With that declaration and nothing better to go on, Rex and Anne were stumped; they didn't know whether to believe Fritz or not, and they didn't have enough probable cause for a search warrant of Fritz's house. That would put Eric Wilkson in charge of the investigation from there. . Ron Belmore skipped out on his rent according to the manager and had associated with a known suspect felon, but not being charged wouldn't be a liable source for the judge to sign a search warrant.

Rex drove a couple blocks away, circled back, and followed the girls and Fritz to see where they went.

"You're going to follow them and see where they go, aren't you?" asked Anne with a knowing smile.

"I'm just making sure they had nothing to do with the kidnapping. Frieda could be in Fritz's house, but we'd need a search warrant to get in."

"Which we don't have right now," replied Anne aggravated.

Rex and Anne followed the girls and Fritz to a park to watch them sit and talk for an hour, and then they went their separate ways; the girls went one way and Fritz the other. Rex chose to follow Fritz, but he returned to his house while Anne followed the girls.

Rex and Anne returned to Rex's house to think things over and decide what to do now.

"What about some of the family, or the family's friends? We haven't checked them out yet," stated Anne.

"No, but right now I am tired and hungry," replied Rex, heading toward the refrigerator to look at leftovers from last night's cookout.

"You're stressed out from not solving this case. Just give it a little time; something will pop up. I'm sure of it," Anne assured Rex.

"I hope so. I don't think we've overlooked anything."

Rex gave Hillary a call to check on him. He was curious as to how things were at the police station.

"You and Anne are on the news about the investigation and going to Balta Street. That was pretty scary, I imagine," stated Hillary. "Eric saw the news, as well, and was stressed out; he'd like to stop you two, but he can't. Karl and Gertrud hired you two to investigate and find their daughter."

"We are stumped right now. We checked out that guy we wondered about, but it looks like he's clean. We tracked him to his house, but we would need a signed search warrant to get in his house, and to do that, we'd need a probable cause. We don't have any cause for a search warrant as of now," stated Rex.

"There's always that legality to deal with, isn't there?"

"It's to protect citizens' rights," replied Rex. "Sometimes, though, it gets in the way of catching the bad guys. Anne and I aren't totally convinced of the four persons-of-interest innocence just yet. We also need to run a check on Karl and Gertrud's family and friends."

"What are you asking, Rex?" asked Hillary, feeling like part of the team.

"I need to know if there's anybody I need to take a closer look at on both sides of the Schumacher family," replied Rex.

"Uh,, okay, I'll have Leeroy take a look at the Schumacher family record to see if there is any shady characters or dirty laundry."

"We're beginning to look anywhere for answers, but nothing questionable turns up," declared Rex.

"That's the way it goes sometimes. Now you know how I felt when I was stumped," replied Hillary.

"I have experienced times like this, but eventually something came around to close the case," replied Rex.

Later in the day, Hillary called Rex back. "Leeroy found a distant bad boy in the family, a brother of a sister-in-law of Karl Schumacher, Boris Kulzer, brother of Katherine Kulzer married to Earl Schumacher, had served six years for assault and battery, and twenty years for rape in the pen. I got his description; he's built like a fullback, 6'4", 280 pounds, light brown hair."

"Where is he now? Do you have an address for him?" asked Rex anxiously.

"His address is 1573 West Brookshire Drive," replied Hillary. "You want me to go with you? He might behave and answer your questions if there are two of us."

"I wish I had reason to question him other than a hunch. I don't know how Karl would take a member of his family becoming a suspect, even if he is a distant relative," stated Rex.

"Being that Boris is a distant relative, if you question him and have reason to suspect him, you could then call Karl," suggested Hillary.

Rex told Anne, and she said she'd like to go along. "If he's in a bar, pub, or some similar place, I could go in disguise to look for him and let you know."

"It may get a little hairy if we confront him and he doesn't want to be questioned, or if he has something to hide," replied Rex.

"I'd stay in the car and let you two handle that."

Hillary, Rex, and Anne drove to Boris's house, but he wasn't home. They drove to the nearest bar, Bud's. Inside, Anne saw him talking to a girl young enough to be his daughter. The girl seemed to be enjoying his company. Anne returned to the car to tell Hillary and Rex.

"Look at that, Anne was right; sweet talking to a girl young enough to be his daughter," replied Hillary, entering the bar with Rex.

"Some guys like them young, and some girls prefer older guys," replied Rex,

Hillary shook his head. Rex and Hillary walked over to Boris and told him they would to talk to him.

"Can't you see I'm busy talking to someone. Bug off! Talk to me later!" snared Boris.

"Yes, we can see you are, but it's best to talk to us now, or we can have Karl Schumacher come talk to you." stated Rex.

With that said, Boris told the girl he'd be back as soon as he got this straightened out. Boris became nervous at the mention of Karl Schumacher. "What's so important?" Boris asked ebulliently.

"You are a person-of-interest in the disappearance of Frieda Schumacher," stated Rex. "Do you know where she is? And don't lie to us!"

"Why would I be a person-of-interest in her disappearance? I don't know where she is!" snared Boris. "You trying to pin that on me?"

"You've served six years for assault and battery, and twenty years for rape, so you are a suspect." stated Rex.

"Not so loud. Yes, I served my time and I have kept myself clean since then, besides, you think I want to do anything that sends me back? You think I want to do anything to Karl's daughter? I intend to stay clean, and for something like that, he could make me disappear permanently," whispered Boris. "What gives you the right to question me? " inquired Boris angrily. "I know Hillary; he got relieved as Police Chief."

"I am Rex Morgan, a private investigator working for Karl and Gertrud Schumacher to find their daughter, Frieda. I have only your word on this. If you don't know where Frieda is, do you have any idea who could've taken her, or where she could have gone?" continued Rex.

"No, whoever took Karl's daughter must have a strong reason, or be very brave, or both, maybe tired of living!" declared Boris. "Frieda is adopted. Karl and Gertrud adopted her when she was six months old, but nobody knows it except the immediate family, and even Frieda doesn't know. I found out only by eavesdropping on a family conversation," replied Boris quietly. "To take Karl's daughter, someone must be tired of living, even if she is adopted!"

"I'll need to confirm this. I suppose the courthouse will have record of it, but that was a long time ago," replied Rex thoughtfully.

"It's possible if Frieda found out, I think it's possible if she traced them and went to see them," replied Boris.

"We need to locate Frieda's real parents and see if she returned to them or went to visit," Rex said to Hillary. "Have you seen any suspicious characters hanging around or driving by Karl and Gertrud's house?" Hillary asked Boris.

"Oh, I saw an old, rusted, green Ford pickup driving slowly one day about eight weeks ago, but they went on, so I didn't think anything of it," stated Boris.

"They? There were two people in the truck, both male and female?" asked Rex anxiously.

"No, there was a young guy and a young girl, late teens or early twenties maybe," stated Boris.

"Can you describe them?" asked Rex anxiously.

"The guy had light brown hair, I think, and the girl had dark hair. I was standing at the curb. You have an ideal who now?" asked Boris.

"I think I might have. They didn't sound convincing when Anne and I questioned them, but there was a guy and three girls," replied Rex. "We didn't have reason to pursue any further questioning."

"They must have had good reason to grab Karl Schumacher's daughter! Darn good reason!" exclaimed Boris. "It wasn't me! Anne, who is Anne, where is she?"

"Oh, she is in the car," replied Rex.

Boris returned to the young girl waiting, but about to give up on Boris.

Leaving, Hillary asked, "You know who they are?"

"I'm pretty sure, but Anne and I have to find out why and prove it." stated Rex. "We'll have to stake them out, see where they go. Fritz's house is of interest now!"

"Fritz?" asked Hillary excited. "There was a guy called Fritz of a questionable character. We never learned his last name. Everybody just called him 'Fritz'."

Anne was told about Frieda being adopted.

"Did you have anything on Fritz?" Rex asked Hillary back in the car with Anne, looking at Hillary excitedly, new hope.

"There were drug and illegal arms deals going on, but the one suspected ringleader got away in a raid," stated Hillary. "The ones caught never knew his real name; he stayed elusive."

"Sounds like it might be Fritz; he meets up with the girls at a café and they talk. We've never been able to listen in on their conversations," stated Anne. "I never was convinced of the girls' innocence."

"Maybe I could get this former client to bug the table at the café," suggested Rex. "Well now, we have two different directions to explore to see which way leads us to Frieda."

"Well, if I can be of any help, just let me know," stated Hillary. "If you bug the girls and Fritz's conversations, you can't use it in court;, it would be fruits of the poisonous tree."

"That is true, but it might let us know if we're on the right track, or if we're wasting our time," stated Rex.

"It wouldn't surprise me if Fritz is tied up some way or other," replied Hillary.

"If Fritz is involved, then I figure the girls are too," declared Anne, Rex and Hillary nodding in agreement.

"We will give you a call sooner or later. I'm sure, you've been a big help in this investigation," stated Rex. Anne agreed. "You could see if you can come up with anything on Fritz, what's his last name, and if Fritz is his real name or just a name he's using."

So the investigation returned to Marina, Nicole, Margret, and Fritz now, only this time, Rex and Anne would stake them out in disguise.

We're onto you now, Anne thought to herself. *If Frieda goes back to visit her real parents, it doesn't go anywhere as far as kidnapping*, Anne thinks to herself.

At the courthouse, Hillary, Rex, and Anne went to the *Births and Deaths* department to check the birth of Frieda, but there was no record of a birth by that name. Then they went the adoption department to check the record to confirm the Schumacher's adoption of Frieda. Sure enough, Frieda had been adopted when she was barely six months old from Catherine and Adrien Fournier. Rex wrote down their name, address, and phone number, in case it was still the same.

Going to the address, it turned out they had moved, and the people living there had no idea where the Fournier family lived.

"Did a real estate handle the transaction?" asked Anne.

"Yes, but that was twenty-two years ago," replied the woman. "I don't remember the real estate's name."

"Well, it will be recorded at the County Board of Registry and Deeds" stated Rex, hopeful.

Arriving at the county board office, they all went to the Registry of Real Estate department to look up the name of the real estate handling the Fournier. There was no real estate involved; Adrien and Catherine had sold the house themselves by placing an ad in the newspaper. The address where they could be located was in the lower eastside part of town that the Brownstone Realty was restoring.

"What do we do now? The Brownstone Realty has bought that property that's been desolate for some years now, and are restoring the entire neighborhood!" exclaimed Rex, stressed, and Anne too.

Hillary was perplexed as what to do too.

"Let's go home for a cookout while we figure out what to do," stated Rex.

"That's what we do when we're stumped," laughed Anne.

Hillary grinned slightly. "Have you given any thought as to what you're going to do now?" asked Hillary after eating.

"An idea came to mind going to the courthouse to see if Frieda had changed her name back to what it was before she was adopted," replied Rex. "Of course, we'd do that tomorrow, unless you two have something in mind," he said, looking at Anne and Hillary.

"What if she is living with her natural parents? Assuming Fritz and the girls haven't got her." asked Anne.

"In that case, we'd have to look for where her parents are living, wherever that might be," replied Rex. "Let's check the courthouse just in case. Start thinking positive, Anne."

"I feel it's best to prepare for the worst while hoping for the best," stated Anne.

"She has a point, Rex," stated Hillary.

"She has a habit of that," replied Rex, smiling.

Anne grinned.

"If Frieda hasn't gone back to her parents, we'll stake out Fritz and the girls."

"What if Hillary and I stake out Fritz and the girls while you check out if Frieda went to her parents?" suggested Anne.

"Well, we could do it that way, but Hillary and Anne, you two behave yourselves while you're out there," Rex teases Hillary.

"I'll ty my best," Hillary replied with a grin, stumped for a second.

Anne laughed.

"I need to call Leo Espanola and have him place electronic bugs under the tables at Aerre's to record Fritz and the girls' conversation," Rex thought to himself and called Leo.

"Sure, I can do that. Ihat will be easier than bugging Alex Spemann's house," replied Leo.

Rex gave Leo the address.

"Thanks, I owe you a favor again," replied Rex.

"I like it that way. I prefer you owing me a favor rather than me owing you one," replied Leo.

The next morning, Rex went to the courthouse to see if Frieda had her name changed back to her birthname "Fournier", but she had not.

Hillary and Anne, in disguise, went to Pierre's Café to wait for Marina, Nicole, Margret, and Fritz.

Now I must locate her natural parents to see if she is living with them, Rex realized. To locate them, being that they no longer lived in the lower eastside would be no easy task, and might be what Frieda wanted. Just to know she was safe and sound was Rex and Anne's goal, and now Hillary too. Hillary had been a huge help in this investigation; it would've been harder without his help.

Anne and I owe him!

Rex decided he'd go to the post office to see if they would give the address of the Fournier family. The post office didn't give such information because of the privacy law.

Rex went to the Schumacher house to give them the latest news.

Karl seemed to accept it pretty well, although a little stressed, but Gertrud sat in the easy chair, folding and unfolding her hands nervously, which Rex noticed. Karl seemed to stay calm, even in stress.

"You don't have any idea who might have a grudge against one of you or Frieda?" asked Rex.

"I have no knowledge of anybody having a grudge against us or Frieda strong enough to pull something like this," stated Karl.

Gertrud shook her head.

"Well, if you think of anything, let us know even if it might seem insufficient, still let us know," stated Rex looking at Karl, wondering.

Karl didn't seem to take it as hard as Gertrud. I wonder if he's not telling us what he knows for some reason. I wonder why they haven't mentioned Frieda's adoption, maybe something to do with that. I wonder if they know she's gone back to her birth parents, but ashamed to say so. So, what if Frieda has gone back to her real parents? No big deal, but maybe to them, it is.

Returning to his house, Rex fixed something to eat quickly to relax and unwind, calling it a day, and waiting on Hillary and Anne to return, hopefully with good news.

Hillary and Anne returned with nothing to report: the girls and Fritz just sat and talked, and then went their separate ways.

"You didn't find out anything. I can tell by your expression," said Anne. "You look beat."

Hillary, tired as well, looked on silently.

"Frieda didn't change back to her birthname. The post office wouldn't give the parents' address because of the privacy law, and Karl and Gertrud didn't seem to know anything more than what they've told us. No mention of Frieda's adoption either," stated Rex. "Well, did you two behave yourselves while you were out?"

"We'll never tell," replied Anne, laughing with Hillary.

Anne decided to spend the night at her house as Hillary said he'd see them later. Anne decided to call it a day with no real results, but wondered why Karl and Gertrud kept quiet about Frieda's adoption. Rex was stressed, as was Anne. She went to her kitchen, had a nightcap, and went to bed, tired.

The next day Hillary felt Anne needed to talk to Gertrud about Frieda's adoption and let her know Rex and her were aware. But why were Karl and Gertrud keeping the secret? If they knew where Frieda's natural parents lived, they needed to tell Rex and Anne. Anne could stress this to Gertrud while Karl and Rex talked in the living room.

Hillary called Rex and expressed this. Rex agreed they needed to let Karl and Gertrud know the adoption was no longer a secret.

"I'll ask Anne to talk to Gertrud about it," replied Rex. Rex called Anne and told her what Hillary suggested. "I agree with Hillary."

"So do I, but if Gertrud will admit it and talk about it," replied Anne. "I wonder why they have kept that a secret with Frieda missing."

"That's a good question. Maybe you could ask her about that; woman-to-woman," stated Rex. "If she won't talk about it, then that would bring their relationship with Frieda into question. I don't think Karl and Gertrud want that."

"True, I'll talk to her and see what she says, if anything," replied Anne.

By luck, Karl wasn't home; he went to talk with friends and play golf.

"Gertrud, the reason I came is so I could talk to you. The other day, Rex and I noticed Karl seemed pretty calm while you were folding and unfolding your hands nervously about us not getting anywhere now. Rex and I know about you adopting Frieda, but you haven't mentioned it. Why have you kept it from us? Do you know where her parents live, so we can see if Frieda is with her parents?" asked Anne.

Gertrud surprised that Rex and Anne knew about the adoption, looked down and then looked away, stressed.

"What is the matter?" asked Anne, wondering. "It's going to come out sooner or later. Rex is good at uncovering the truth and bringing it out into the open. I'm pretty good too. Rex won't let this go away, not now!"

"We suspect she had discovered who her birth parents were and gone to them. She and Boris might have had an affair, and to avoid any friction in our family, and bringing shame on us as well herself, we think she went back to her birth parents. Our friends would be shocked at such a scandalous mess!" declared Gertrud stressed. "Karl wouldn't show his face at the country club it would he such a scandal!"

"Well, I guess in high society that wouldn't be something you'd want revealed, but it's becoming more common and accepted these days. I would think of my daughter and stand up for her first, even if she was adopted, over any society image." declared Anne, a bit surprised, but not really.

Anne and Rex felt there was something being kept from them, but it was out. in high society of tire elite! With that over and uncovered, Gertrud was stressed and Anne, feeling sorry for her, tried to console her.

"Do you think she'll ever come back?" asked Anne, concerned for Gertrud.

"I don't know. Maybe to visit, but not to live here. Karl hasn't figured out what to do about Boris; leave it alone, or take care of Boris.

Of course he wouldn't do it himself," stated Gertrud.

"But he could go to prison for that!" exclaimed Anne.

"If he was caught, but he wouldn't do it himself," replied Gertrud. "Oh, there is one other thing you might as well know, you'll probably find out anyway. There is a close friend of Karl's from the country club, more like a brother who had helped Karl get started in the business world, and he was drunk one night and messed with Frieda in a frolic manner. Frieda laughed it off, him chasing her around the house, but then he left. He had a thing for her, if you know what I mean, but Karl doesn't think he had anything to do with her disappearance. He refuses to believe it, that is why we didn't tell you."

"Karl just might be surprised. We have to know his name and address so we can check and clear him or not," stated Anne. "Do you have a picture of this friend? If not, I need a description of him."

Gertrud went to a writing desk for a picture of him and Karl together, giving it to Anne.

"His name is Heinrich Ottoman. He used to live in Hinder Brooks Estates, but I don't know if he's still there or not," answered Gertrud wearily. "But Karl believes he is innocent. I guess because Heinrich helped Karl get started and they are such close friends."

"Well, we have to check him out to see if he is as good and close friend as Karl thinks," stated Anne. "As far as Karl not taking care of Boris himself, but have it done, under the law he would be just as guilty because he had it done. That is the law. Are you going to be okay?"

"Yeah, being it's out now. I knew it would come out eventually with Rex and you on the case. I'll be okay. I don't think Karl will do anything, as far as Boris is concerned. I'm sure of it. I may lie down a while," replied Gertrud tired.

Anne excused herself and left to report back to Rex with maybe a breakthrough. Now, first we check out the girls and Fritz.

Anne arrived back at Rex's house to get something to eat and relay what Gertrud had told her. Hearing this, Rex was surprised how it turned out, but figured there was something Karl and Gertrud were holding back. Anne fixed herself a sandwich, chips, and a tall glass of sweetened ice tea, went on the deck to eat, relax, and unwind. Rex went out to join her relaxing.

"Well now, we have to check out Heinrich Ottoman to see how close a friend he is to Karl," stated Rex.

Rex decided to have Hillary call his police friend to run a check on Heinrich Ottoman. "He used to live in Hider Brooks Estates. We don't know if he still lives there or not."

"Ah, another person-of-interest?" asked Hillary anxiously.

"It looks that way," replied Rex.

"Helping you out for a change, things aren't so boring now. I'm glad I can help," stated Hillary.

"We're glad too. You've been an immense help many times," replied Rex.

After Rex hung up, Leo Espanola called.

"Rex, I have those tapes from the café. There are some interesting and questionable statements made. I'd say they are persons-of-interest, as you call it," stated Leo.

"Oh good. I'll be over to pick them up," replied Rex.

Rex told Anne what Leo said as Anne listened anxiously, but not really surprised. "Well, now we have the girls and Fritz and Heinrich Ottoman as suspects.. Is there any room for more?" asked Rex amused.

Anne grinned.

Rex drove over to pick up the tapes as Anne decided to stay put, relax, and enjoy the backyard; she was tired from all this pursuing and questioning. Leo handed Rex the tapes and told him his sister and his brother-in-law separated for a while and then got back together, now going for counseling.

"Good, I'm glad to hear that! I'm always glad to hear good reports!" declared Rex. "Now, I owe you for these tapes."

"I'll let you know if I need your help," replied Leo.

The next day, Hillary called Rex to tell him Leeroy ran a check on Heinrich Ottoman, but the file clerk told Leeroy there was nothing on Ottoman, but he doesn't believe her because she had a suspicious expression of not looking Leeroy straight in the face. Leeroy had the feeling she wasn't telling the truth, but he didn't know why.

"Does Ottoman have a friend or connections in the police department?" asked Rex puzzled.

"It looks that way. It might be something to consider. Call Wayne Milton and talk to him?" asked Hillary.

"I can, but all we have is a suspicion, nothing really sustainable to go on," stated Rex. "I suggest we locate this Heinrich Ottoman to see where he lives and tail him wherever he goes, but don't say a word to anybody about it. It's time to go to ground with this investigation and see what or who turns up!"

"Sounds good to me. This is exciting! Sure beats sitting around the house watching TV all day!" declared Hillary.

"You get your job back, you'll stay busy then."

"Whenever that is, and if I get back," replied Hillary. "I'm waiting."

"Oh, I'm confident you will. Erie isn't doing too good a job at impressing Wayne Milton, I don't think," stated Rex, grinning.

Rex told Anne his conversation with Hillary, and she agreed it was time to go to ground, not saying a word to anybody.

"What do you think of taking this hush-hush on Ottoman to Wayne Milton or Cheryl Nickels the District Attorney and have them to run a check on Heinrich Ottoman to see what comes up?" Rex asked Anne.

"You could do that. We'd know if Leeroy is leveling with us or playing us," stated Anne.

Rex and Anne drove to Wayne Milton's office to run a check on Heinrich Ottoman. He had a shady past, but nothing concrete. Wayne said after running the name through the files. He had never been to trail just questioned about a covert operation in Columbia.

Wayne wanted to know why Rex and Anne were interested in Heinrich Ottoman. Rex and Anne lay out their investigation. Wayne understood why they were interested.

"You two go wherever the lead takes you. Didn't you know going to Balta Street was a dangerous idea?" lectured Wayne Milton.

"We knew, but we were looking for Loui Binoche, but he never showed. We feel he was in there somewhere, but we didn't dare go looking for him," stated Rex.

"You can be glad you didn't find him; he is not a nice guy to deal with, much less question!" declared Wayne Milton.

"We knew that when we went but that was where the lead on him took us and lucky we came out alive," replied Rex. Wayne just shook his head, Rex and Anne smiling.

Rex and Anne decided to see what Cheryl Nickels had to say. She pretty much said the same thing Wayne Milton said. Well now, it was confirmed Heinrich Ottoman had friends in the police department and maybe other places as well.

"All we can do is tail them," stated Rex and Anne agreed. "Frieda has to be somewhere, but is she alive or dead? That is the sixty-four-dollar question! You have any ideas?" Rex asked Anne.

"Not at the moment, but if we put our heads together, we'll come up with something. I'm sure of it," replied Anne.

Rex and Anne decided to locate and tail Heinrich Ottoman to see who showed and where he went, but Rex needed his camera equipment and went to get it.

"With Heinrich's picture, we can look for him in the Binder Brooks Estates if he's still there and stake him out to see who shows up and where he goes, and I can get their picture," stated Rex.

"We may be surprised," replied Anne. "Maybe another person-of-interest," stated Anne jokingly.

Rex grinned and shook his head. "So be it, it's time we start making some headway soon now!" declared Rex.

Driving to the Hinder Brook Estates and driving slowly around the community they didn't see Heinrich. maybe he was inside his house or else he's gone somewhere or moved. Finally, Rex pulled to a stop and waited a while as Anne and he sat and watched the houses. After an hour, Rex drove around slowly and spotted Heinrich in his yard looking at his rose bushes. Rex stopped a block away, taking a close-up with 55mm zoom lens of Heinrich in his yard, Rex and Anne sat and watched if anyone showed up. Later that afternoon, Fritz pulled in Heinrich's driveway and got out talking to Heinrich as Rex clicked their picture, using his 55mm zoom lens for a close-up.

"Well, well, looks like Fritz knows Heinrich Ottoman. I wonder what they have in common and talk about!" stated Rex.

"Would be interesting to find out if we had a way," replied Anne. "Fritz always was the type who seemed to keep secrets and never be upfront with you."

"Maybe if I ran his picture in the FBI files, they might pull up something," stated Rex.

"I figure he's the type who stays in the background of anything going down to avoid answering questions, being arrested and avoided his picture to show in the files," replied Anne.

"Oh, he's slick alright. I wonder if the girls are in with these two or not and what they are into," asked Rex puzzled.

"I feel the girls are probably involved in some way or other. I don't think they're the innocent type, but I suspect Fritz is the main man," stated Anne.

"I suspect that as well, but they are all lying low in whatever is going on. I suspect Frieda is around somewhere, we just need to find her," declared Rex.

Rex and Anne continued to watch Heinrich and Fritz as they continued to talk, then going into Heinrich's house, Rex took their picture. An hour later, Heinrich and Fritz emerged and drove over to Fritz's house and went inside. Again, Rex took their picture from a block away.

"Well, well, how about that?" exclaimed Rex excited. "I don't know if the District Attorney or the Attorney General will need these pictures, but it will show Fritz and Heinrich as cozy friends into something," declared Rex.

"I wonder what or who is inside that house, but we'd have to have probable cause to get a signed search warrant and we don't have that yet. I have a hunch, but hunches don't count!" stormed Anne angrily.

"Gotta' have a really good reason signed by a judge to get inside, and then only with Wayne Elton, Cheryl Nickels, or Altos Bradley present," stated Rex.

"Or Eric Wilkson," teased Anne. Rex made a face, and then Anne laughed. "We're going to have to do something to get a search warrant!" stated Anne, frustrated.

As they waited, they listened to the tapes Leo Espanola illegally obtained. What they heard was a bit of surprise. What did they know about 11-165 and automatic fire rifles, Mi6A2 and AR-15 and sniper rifles? They didn't say they had them, but talked about them, as if they were getting them soon. That was a violation by itself.

Rex and Anne sat waiting for something to happen. An hour later, Marina, Nicole, and Margret showed up and went into Fritz's house without knocking. Rex got their picture going into the house. After listening to the tape, maybe the girls, Heinrich and Fritz could be in a conspiracy involving illegal guns.

"Wow, well, the girls, Heinrich, and Fritz must all be involved together in whatever is going on!" declared Rex.

"The girls have been here before," replied Anne.

"Yes, but Heinrich is here too this time. Whatever is going on, the girls must be involved, I am sure of it now!" exclaimed Rex.

"I'm sure of it too, but how do we find out?" asked Anne anxiously.

Rex called Wayne Milton to play the tape and relay how the investigation was going so far. Wayne was surprised Rex obtained another illegal tape, but was surprised wheat was on the tape. Wayne said he felt whatever was happening was in Fritz's house as well, but the tape couldn't be used in court. Rex and Anne hadn't figure out what was going on as of yet.

"Sounds suspicions alright, but we need a good reason for probable cause signed by a judge to go inside the house," declared Wayne Milton. "If the persons-of-interest just came out by themselves, and there's no sign of Frieda, then the suspects are just suspects, nothing more."

"Yeah, I know," replied Rex, discouraged.

"Just keep up the surveillance around the house, and don't get caught. They'll know you're onto them. Keep me informed and maybe we can come up with something," suggested Wayne. "If you see Frieda, then we have reason for to go in the house and arrest the suspects."

"Maybe something will happen or break soon. Is what you're saying?" asked Rex.

"Yes, just observe who comes, goes, and what they do, if anything," replied Wayne Milton, hoping.

"Okay, I understand," replied Rex, who told Anne what the police director said.

Wayne called Milton Bradley and Cheryl Nickels to let them know Rex Morgan and Anne Towers maybe is about to expose the kidnapping case of Frieda and tell about the illegal tape Rex received from a former client."

Wayne Milton, Milton Bradley, and Cheryl Nickels were surprised Rex obtained another useful, but illegal tape, and yet excited to wait for Rex's call in the District Attorney's Conference Room. Wayne called

Jan Roberts and Harold Jacobs; they were excited hearing about Rex and Anne. They, along with the camera crew, now anxiously wait for Rex's call as well.

"Right now, they are waiting for something to happen or if they see Frieda."

Jan and Harold understood.

"So, all we do is sit and wait!" replied Anne after listening to what Wayne Milton told Rex.

"They're waiting anxiously for things to start happening, same as us, and so we wait!"

"We wait until something happens or we see Frieda, then I call Wayne Milton back so they can make the arrest and rescue Frieda," replied Rex, hopeful.

"Then the reporters will be here as well for a 6:00 hot news bulletin, and the whole neighborhood will be watching as well," stated Anne amused.

"You got that right," replied Rex, smiling. "Wayne will probably call Eric Wilkson so he can be here, probably to watch."

"Oh, he'll have a few things to say to us," stated Anne.

"You can count on it," replied Rex dryly.

Rex and Anne sat, watching and waiting for something to happen or see Frieda with or without the crew. Rex and Anne had about given up when Heinrich, Fritz, and the girls step outside the door. Rex quickly snapped their picture. Then Rex and Anne saw Frieda peek out the window. Rex looked through the zoom lens of his camera and saw her; her face looked puffy and swollen and she held her left arm. Fritz, looking back, saw her in the window and rushed back into the house.

"Joy comes to those who wait!" declared Rex excited.

Anna grinned and was excited as well. Rex quickly called Wayne and told him. "We saw Frieda peeking out the window, but Fritz, seeing her, rushed back in the house! Frieda's face looked puffy and swollen and she was holding her left arm!"

"Alright, we'll be right there; don't let them leave. Detain them by talking to them."

Cheryl and John jumped up in excitement.

Wayne called Jan Roberts and Harold Jacobs. "Rex and Anne saw Frieda! Rex and Anne are going over to talk to them until we get there!"

Jan and Harold were excited and rushed for the van with the camera crew.

"Let's talk to them and keep them here until Wayne Milton, Cheryl, and Milton Bradley get here," Rex told Anne.

Rex and Anne quickly drove up to the house, got out, and said, "Hello."

"Who are they? I don't know them," declared Heinrich.

The girls were surprised and a bit scared. Fritz came out surprised and a bit confused. Rex and Anne remove their disguises.

"What are you two doing here? Haven't we told you everything we know? Why are you here?" demanded Fritz.

"We weren't aware you knew, Heinrich. You're a friend of Karl and Gertrud Schumacher, aren't you, Heinrich?" Rex asked.

"Yeah, so what if I am?" demanded Heinrich.

"We didn't know you were friends with Marina, Nicole, Margret, and Fritz," stated Anne.

"Big deal, so what? How is that any of your business?"

"We saw Frieda peeking out the window; her face looked puffy and swollen and she was holding her left arm!" declared Rex. "Karl won't like that!"

"Who are you two? Why are you questioning us?" demanded Heinrich alarmed.

"I am Rex Morgan, and she is my assistant, Anne Towers. We are investigating the disappearance of Frieda Schumacher, Karl and Gertrud want her back!"

Heinrich looked panicked.

Frieda, hearing Karl and Gertrud and her name mentioned, staggered to the door holding her arm, her face puffy and swollen. Anne rushed to catch Frieda and helped her out of the door.

In the distance, drawing closer were the sirens and flashing lights as Wayne Milton, Cheryl Nickels, Milton Bradley, and Larry Flippant, along with the police, came bearing down the street with the ABC and NBC news reporters right behind them. Behind them are Karl and Gertrud Schumacher. By now, the neighbors start coming out to watch.

"What do we do now? We're dead in the water!" declared Heinrich, depressed as well.

Fritz and the girls stand there like three suspects knowing they were caught, but not knowing what to do!

Jan and Harold, along with the camera crew with their cameras rolling, report as officers approached to arrest Heinrich Ottoman, Fritz, Marina, Nicole, and Margret and took them into custody. Their rights were read to them as the girls tried to hide their faces. Fritz, looking defiant, appeared as though he thought about running, but realized it would be useless.

"Why did you kidnap Frieda Schumacher?" asked Anne.

"You wouldn't understand," replied Heinrich mournfully.

"You might as well try, you'll be talking to the FBI and the police, and kidnapping is a federal offense! We're waiting and listening!"

"We're not talking; we have nothing to say to you!" snarled Fritz to Rex and Anne as he, Heinrich, and the girls were led to waiting cruisers.

The news cameras took it all in. The girls were about to breakdown. Frieda was led over to Karl and Gertrud.

Karl, seeing Heinrich in handcuffs, rage rushed over to him. "How could you? I thought we were friends! How could you?" blurted out Karl, ready to fight. The scene was being recorded on camera as well for the evening news.

"I…I'm sorry…I'm so sorry" stammered Heinrich.

"Well, that just isn't enough!" snared Karl and returned to Gertrud and Frieda.

Eric Wilkson saw Rex and Anna and came bearing over to demand why the police weren't called until the last moment.

Rex and Anne braced themselves for the stern, verbal assault.

"I want to know why you haven't called to report these suspects! You are supposed to report any suspicious activity or persons to the police!" snarled Eric.

"We had persons-of-interest, but not enough to classify them as suspects, and besides, you told Anne and I you would solve your own cases' you don't need outside help, our help. You told us that!" declared Rex.

At that moment, Wayne Milton, overhearing Eric and Rex's feud, walked over to inform Eric Rex and Anne had kept in touch with him with all suspicious behavors.

"They came to you but not me? I am the Chief of Police!" declared Eric.

"Yes, but you told them you would solve your own cases and didn't need their help. You had the police force to help you, if needed." declared Wayne. "Persons-of-interest aren't liable to report until they give us probable cause, or commit some offense."

"I still feel they should have come to me anyway," replied Eric, but saw he was getting nowhere and in an embarrassing fix, so he backed off. Eric realized he went too far in arrogantly telling Rex and Anne he would solve his own cases. He didn't know the police force was that untrained. There was nothing that could change that now. He didn't know Rex and Anne were that good at solving cases, but now he did.

Wayne Milton turned to Jan Roberts, Harold Jacobs, and the camera crew to make a statement, moving so Fritz's house was in full view. Wayne motioned for Rex and Anne to join him, along with Cheryl Nickels and Milton Bradley. "As for now, these people taken into custody will be charged with kidnapping until we get further into the investigation and question the suspects to obtain more information. This house is an official crime scene," declared Wayne Milton.

Officials taped off the front and back of the house and put a lock on the front and back doors as it was recorded on the news camera.

Wayne went over to Frieda to tell her they'd need to talk about all that went on and the reason Heinrich, Fritz, and the girls kidnapped her.

Karl asked if that could wait in time for Frieda to get checked out and treated at the hospital, and Wayne agreed, but they'd need a report from the hospital as well. Karl and Gertrud acknowledged agreement.

"They were hoping to get money from Dad and Mom to buy and move a shipment of M-I6s, some automatic rapid-fire rifles and M24 bolt action and Knights SR-25 carbine sniper rifles to Columbia to a rebel group," muttered Frieda, barely able to speak. "They had a buyer. There had been an faded green truck following me, and Fritz and the girls offered to hide me out," she muttered.

"We'll need you to sign a statement to the prosecutor, then testify in court after you have recovered enough to do so," stated Wayne Milton, with Cheryl Nickels listening intently.

"But not today, right?" asked Karl. "She needs time to recover, and we need a little time to ourselves."

"Oh no, not today, but as soon as possible," stated Cheryl Nickels. "We'll keep in touch. If you see any suspicious characters, call us immediately!"

"I understand," replied Frieda weakly. "A week would be okay to make a statement."

Karl and Gertrud nodded in agreement.

"Okay, we'll see you in a week or so?" asked Cheryl.

"Later part of the morning preferably, after I have my coffee and breakfast," replied Frieda with a smile.

"Oh yeah, gotta have that morning coffee," replied Cheryl with a laugh. "We better let her be for now, her voice is starting to go and she's getting weaker. Have her checked out at the hospital."

Wayne, Cheryl, and John went into Fritz's house to get a layout of the house and gather evidence to present to the defense and court for a trail. In a bottom drawer was a voucher for three caches of M-I6s, Mi6A2, AR-I5 automatic rapid-fire rifles and M24 bolt action and Knights SR-25 carbine sniper rifles and ammunition from an arms ammunition supply company. That would raise the charge to kidnapping, conspiracy to purchase illegal firearms, and attempt to transport illegal firearms overseas for a revolution. That would set them up for several years, maybe even life. The supplier would be charged as well. Picking up the voucher by the tip, it was put into a small forensic bag later to be dusted for fingerprints and checked out the company selling these illegal firearms. Also, there was a long-distance phone number on a piece of paper, which was put in a forensic bag to be dusted for fingerprints. On the desk, a typewriter was dusted for fingerprints and taken to compare the ransom note sent to Karl and Gertrud, and to see what was on the tape. The typing paper was taken as well to compare the paper to the those of the ransom notes. In the basement were the rifles and ammunition in crates, ready to ship. Those was loaded into vans to be taken to FBI headquarters as evidence.

At the jail, Heinrich, Fritz, Marina, Nicole, and Margret were fingerprinted and their pictures taken, although Fritz had to be forcibly persuaded to cooperate. Heinrich and Fritz were put in separate cells from the girls to wait for their lawyers and to be questioned.

Rex and Anne, returning home, had a late lunch out on the deck. There was a knock on the door.

"Who could that be? Hillary, or the news reporters?" pondered Rex aloud, as he went to the door.

"Well, did the two of you cover the news!" exclaimed Hillary excited. "There was a newsflash that just came on TV about the arrest of

Heinrich, Fritz, and those girls at Fritz's house! There were squad cars all over the street, with neighbors watching as well! You two don't stop until you catch the suspects, do you?" Hillary declared, laughing.

"The investigation is over when the suspects are caught and arrested," replied Rex, grinning with Anne.

"I'm glad it's over," stated Anne. "I, for one, need rest and time to relax and enjoy my house!"

"Eric came over and started in on us for not coming to the police station to turn over what we had discovered, but I told him all we had up to the last moment were suspicions," stated Rex. "Then Wayne Milton came over to confirm my story, and pointed out Eric said he'd would solve his own cases. Erie backed off then."

"Oh, he was upset you two solved the case instead of him! You two spent a great deal of time on the case and went wherever the lead led, and I doubt seriously he would've gone to Balta Street without an army! I wonder how Eric rates with Wayne Milton now?" stated Hillary, grinning.

Rex and Anne laughed knowing what Hillary meant.

"Just give it a little time and we'll see," replied Rex with a mischievous grin.

Just before six o'clock, Rex turned on the TV to watch the news with Hillary and Anne. Heinrich, Fritz, and the three girls were shown being cuffed and led to waiting squad cars. Frieda was led over to Karl and Gertrud and being embraced. Rex and Anne stood on the sideline watching during the arrests and the reunion of Frieda with Karl and Gertrud. Then Karl went to Heinrich to yell at him and ready to fight. There was a view of Fritz's house being taped off and padlocked, then Wayne Milton made a statement with Cheryl Nickels, John Cotter, with Rex and Anne standing with Wayne Milton.

Now, nothing could change that! Eric went to a party store to buy a pint of Jack Daniels and went home to start drinking in deep depression, figuring his career as Police Chief was in shambles! Rex and Anne had made him look like a third-rate amateur, to say the least! He should have kept his job as the assistant, but now…

"Well, I feel, or should I say, I have a hunch you can start on getting your job back soon," stated Rex. "I feel you're their best candidate."

"Oh, that would be great! I don't think I'll be in a big hurry accepting it; let them sweat a little first," replied Hillary. "I think I'll ask for a raise in pay, better medical coverage, more vacation time, and a better retirement package if they ask me to come back."

"Oh, you're going to stick it to them, huh?" asked Rex and Anne, laughing.

"I could use a raise in pay to get a nicer house in a nicer neighborhood. Where I live now is okay. I don't figure I'll ever have a house like in this neighborhood, but it would be nice to have a nicer house than what I have. My car needs replacing; it's old and need repair from time to time and my medical coverage isn't the greatest! I figure I'm in a better position to demand it, thanks to you two!" stated Hillary smiling.

"Then it's time to upgrade, and you deserve it! We're glad to help!" declared Rex, Anne agreeing.

"Well, I sure appreciate it. Maybe if I get my job back, I can afford a better living standard," replied Hillary.

"We'll be able to call you 'Captain' again," stated Anne.

The next week, Hillary called Rex and Anne to tell them he was back as Chief of Police, and they gave him everything he wanted.

Rex was overjoyed to hear that. "Congratulations, Chief. I'm glad to hear it!" declared Rex. "I'll have to call Anne and tell her."

"She's at home enjoying her deck and patio, I suppose. I can't blame her. I would too, but I could use a nicer house, and they teased me about wanting a house like yours or Anne's. I told them I need a new car and better medical coverage, more vacation time, and I could use a better retirement package, and they said that was okay," stated Captain Hillary. "They jokingly accused me of taking advantage of the situation."

"What happened to Erie Wilkson? Did he retire or get fired?"

"They gave him a nice retirement package, and he happily accepted it, figuring he was lucky to get that. They didn't say how much, and neither did he. He told me I can have that job!" replied Captain Hillary. "He said he's moving to another state."

"That was a nice send-off for him, not the way I would want to retire, but it's better than being fired," stated Rex.

Rex called Anne and told her of his call from Captain Hillary. "It's back to Captain Hillary now. They gave Eric a nice retirement package, and he told Hillary he's moving to another state."

"Oh, alright, everything worked out fine. I'm glad to hear that!" replied Anne happily. "I'm glad Eric got a nice retirement package instead of the shaft."

"Yeah, I'm glad. I'm ready for a break before another case," stated Rex. Anne agreed. "All of this excitement is too much for one day; let's spread it out over a few days."

"What do you say we invite Captain Hillary over to celebrate his return as Police Chief and invite Cheryl Nickels, Wayne Milton, John Cotter, and Larry Flippant over as well, or is that too much?" asked Rex.

"Sounds good. Call Captain Hillary and see if he's busy."

"I don't mind if you don't mind the crowd," replied Captain Hillary happily.

Captain Hillary, Cheryl Nickels, John Cotter, Wayne Milton, and Larry Flippant arrived to celebrate Captain Hillary's return to office as Chief of Police.

Anne called Gertrud to see if they wanted to come over for the cookout as well.

Gertrud asked Karl and Frieda if she felt up to it. Gertrud, coming back, said, "Sure, we'd be happy to come."

Shortly after Karl, Gertrud, and Frieda arrived, Jan Roberts from ABC and Harold Jacobs from NBC and their camera crews arrived to capture everybody on camera for the evening news.

"So, Hillary is back in as Chief of Police and Frieda Schumacher has been found and returned home, now recovering well," declared Jan Roberts. "This is something to celebrate!"

Karl, Frieda, and Gertrud posed on the deck as cameras click away.

"How does it feel to be home again?" asked Harold Jacobs. "

"It feels great," declared Frieda happily.

"Could we interview you sometime or other on the kidnapping?" asked Jan Roberts.

"Maybe sometime later. Right now I want to continue to heal and recover emotionally, relax and unwind, and be with my family and friends, for now," stated Frieda.

Cheryl Nickels stated that they had the hospital report of Frieda's injuries and assault and it would be used in the trial.

"Oh, we have Captain Hillary too, he has been a huge help on this case," stated Rex.

Anne agreed as Rex pulled Hillary up beside the two of them as cameras clicked away. Hillary shook his head happily.

"Congratulations on your return to Chief of Police, Captain Hillary!" declared Jan Roberts as everybody clapped.

"Thank you, I am happy to be back! I have missed being Chief!" stated Captain Hillary.

"I bet you have. Apparently, Eric Wilkson was the wrong man for the job, this kidnapping case proved that," stated Harold Jacobs.

"Being Chief isn't the easiest job in the world, but I enjoyed it, and Rex Morgan and Anne Towers have been a big help!" replied Captain Hillary.

"You will be sworn in day after tomorrow," declared Wayne Milton, again clapping.

"Now for another picture of you, Captain Hillary, with Rex Morgan and Anne Towers," requested Jan as cameras started to click.

"I'd like to have a copy for my office as well," requested the Captain.

Rex and Anne each requested a copy as well.

"You each shall have a copy,," declared Jan.

"Thank you."

"Oh, by the way, that subdivision on the lower eastside is almost completed and the housing administration is taking applications of the former residence who lived there, but there are rules and restrictions on moving in, I understand," stated Harold Jacobs.

"Yeah, they will have to keep their houses looking nice: no junky cars, motor cycles sitting in the front or backyards, no junk piled up, and the yards have to be kept up as well," stated Rex. "They have to sign a contract to get a house over there, and it's to the lower income people who used to live there only! The housing administration doesn't want the houses and neighborhood looking like it used to."

"Oh, alright!" replied Jan and Harold together, clapping.

"I want to shake Rex and Anne's hands in appreciation for finding and rescuing our daughter, Frieda," stated Karl, handing Rex a check and shaking Rex and Anne's hands. He whispered to Anne, "That is for you too, Anne."

Anne grinned and said, "Thank you." The news cameras recorded it.

Rex and Anne looked at the check, $150,000.00. "Karl says that is for me too," stated Anne with a grin.

"Ah, I thought that was just for me," replied Rex with a teasing grin.

Anne laughed, shaking her head.

"I have a token of appreciation for Captain Hillary for so graciously helping us," Karl said, and handed Captain Hillary a check for $50,000.00.

Hillary, looking at the check, was in total shock, but happy. Again, the news cameras recorded everything.

"I hardly know what to say, I am truly grateful. I don't feel I helped all that much!" replied Captain Hillary, looking at the check.

Captain Hillary, Karl, Gertrud, Frieda, Rex, Anne, Cheryl Nickels, Wayne Milton, Milton Bradley, and Larry Flippant start out on the deck as Jan, Harold, and the camera crew start to leave, but Rex caught them.

"Aren't you staying to join us for a cookout?" asked Rex confused.

"We didn't want to intrude," replied Jan, but Rex insisted they stay and Anne motioned to come on out on the deck.

"I am ready for this cookout. I am hungry!" declared Hillary.

Rex fired up the grill as Anne, Gertrud, Frieda, and Jan bring meats and food to the grill, then prepared salads, fruit cocktail, potato salad, baked beans, and baked banana pudding and cookies. They all were in a celebration mood of Captain Hillary's return as Police Chief and Frieda Schumacher returning home!

"Exactly what are Heinrich, Fritz, and those girls are charged with, other than kidnapping?" asked Karl.

"Well, I'm not the District Attorney, just the assistant. First, we have to find out how involved each one was involved. I feel Heinrich and Fritz might be the main ones, especially Fritz! I don't think Fritz is his real name, or else he's not giving his last name so we won't know who he really is, but we'll find out," stated Cheryl Nickels. "I don't think Fritz or Heinrich will get bail. If Fritz does, he'll get away for sure. The final decision is up to the District Attorney, Peter Toberman. He's not much for Lindsey in cases like this. I figure he'll want to go the whole nine yards on Fritz."

"The illegal firearms and shipping to a country will be a big issue, as well as the kidnapping; that is a federal offense, and so is kidnapping," FBI Director, Milton Bradley said between bites of food. "I don't know much about the girls yet, how involved they were, but I figure Heinrich and Fritz will do life, especially Fritz."

"I saw Heinrich at the country club. We'd talk and sometimes play golf together, and he never let on he was involved in anything. He was calm and cool like everything was okay," stated Karl Schumacher. "I would never have suspected him."

Eric Wilkson, we gave him a nice retirement package, so there would be no ruckus about bringing back Captain Hillary, he'd just leave quietly and that would be that," stated Wayne Milton.

He was lucky to get whatever he got, I'd say" declared Rex. "He didn't do much that I could see. I am glad for him though, that he didn't get the shaft."

"That's true, he didn't, and it didn't take us long to see he wasn't qualified for the job, but we decided to be nice in offering him a nice retirement package," replied Wayne. "We're glad to have Captain Hillary back!"

"Thank you, I'm glad you feel that way, and I am glad to be back!" replied Captain Hillary.

"Hey, are we having a celebration, or discussing a case? Let's celebrate!" declared Rex.

"The suspects have been arrested, but not convicted yet," corrected Cheryl Nickels.

"Let's forget about the investigation, arrests, and trail for now and celebrate this food while we're together," declared Anne.

"I'm all for that," stated Rex, with everybody nodding in agreement. "Jan and Harold have been quiet over there."

"Just listening and enjoying the food," Jan pat her stomach.

Harold nodded in agreement.

Rex and Anne received an invitation to the official swearing in of Captain Hillary as the Chief of Police and celebration afterward. Rex and Anne arrived at the police headquarters to be greeted by Jan Roberts and Harold Jacobs and the camera crew. Rex noticed Sgt. Judy Sturgis was standing with someone he didn't recognize. Seeing Rex and Anne, Judy took his arm and led him to Rex and Anne.

"Rex and Anne, I'd like you to meet Kory Bishop, my fiancé", declared Judy Sturgis proudly.

"Congratulations!" declared Rex and Anne happily.

Kory shook hands with Rex and Anne.

"Pleased to meet you. I've heard a lot about you both," stated Kory.

"I hope it was good stuff you heard, and we're happy for you," stated Anne.

"Thank you."

Wayne steps to the podium to announce the swearing in of Captain Hillary and everyone quieted down.

"We are here to swear in our Captain Hillary as Chief of Police. We made the mistake of giving him a leave of absence, but it gave him time to rest up and do some things he wanted to get caught up on," stated Wayne Milton, with cameras clicking. "Anything interesting you want to share with us?"

Hillary grinned, and the crowd roared with laughter. Hillary shook his head, jokingly, saying he'd never tell as the crowd continued laughing.

With Captain Hillary sworn in as the Chief of Police, everybody clapped, and he was allowed to say a few words.

"I got caught on some things that needed taking care of, and would have been bored if Rex Morgan and Anne Towers hadn't kept me up-to-date on this kidnapping case by asking for my advice. I am so happy to be back! Anything more than that…" said Captain Hillary jokingly as the crowd roared with laughter.

Wayne Milton shook his finger teasingly. Rex and Anne laughed, while cameras clicked away.

With that, Captain was led over to a table for a ceremonial toast with Peter Toberman, Cheryl Nickels, Milton Bradley, Wayne Milton, and Larry Flippant.

"Come on, Rex Morgan and Anne Towers, we want you up here to join us. You brought this on in bringing Captain Hillary back as Chief of Police," declared Wayne Milton.

Rex and Anne stepped up to the table, each taking a glass of chardonnay to toast Captain Hillary.

"This is a day I'll never forget. I am so happy to be back! You two and I will always be buddies, and I hope it stays that way!" declared Captain Hillary to Rex and Anne.

"So do we!" declared Anne happily. "So do we!"

"Did you meet Sgt. Judy's fiancé yet? He's a nice guy, studying to be a lawyer and I understand he's going to be useful tool," stated Hillary.

"We met. Judy introduced him to us, but she didn't say anything about that," replied Rex happily.

"He's a bit shy about that; he doesn't want to appear boastful. He thinks the world of her, and she feels the same way about him too," stated Captain Hillary.

"That's always good!" stated Rex.

The would-be buyer of the illegal guns wasn't happy about the raid and that he didn't get what he hoped. "Brooks" figured somebody owed him big time, and he intended to collect! He didn't come here to go back emptyhanded, to promise Brooks something and not carry through on it is very bad business!

A lawyer went to see Fritz and ask where the guns were; Brooks was promised a big shipment of M-I6s and Mi6A2, AR-I5 automatic rapid-fire rifles, sniper rifles, plus the ammunition. And when Brooks wanted something, he got it!

Fritz told the lawyer the police and FBI took them in a raid. The lawyer was fuming

"Where and how is Brooks supposed to get those guns promised to him now that you're in here and the FBI and police have them? You don't make promises to Brooks you can't keep!"

"I wasn't expecting a raid. That Rex Morgan and Anne Towers are very good in uncovering things. They were looking for Frieda Schumacher and discovered us. We were caught in the raid with the guns and ammunition," stated Fritz.

"That may be your excuse, but it won't be good enough for Brooks,

I can tell you that now! You're in here, but Brooks can still reach you; he has friends, even in here, and one of them just might come pay you a visit." declared the lawyer with a smirk.

"Just how am I supposed to get his guns and ammunition to him while I'm in here?" fumed Fritz.

"That is your problem, buddy-boy! I pity you."

After the lawyer left, Fritz put in a request to see his lawyer, Burt Sterns, soon as possible. Burt Sterns came to see what was up with Fritz.

"What's up? Your request to talk to me seemed urgent."

"I just had a visit from Brooks' lawyer, and he stated Brooks isn't happy with me about his guns and ammunition owed to him and some goon in here may come visit me! You've got to get me out of here and under protective custody!" exclaimed Fritz. "If you don't, I'm dead!"

"I'll go right now and talk to Cheryl Nickels."

Sterns drove straight to Cheryl's office and told the receptionist it was urgent. The receptionist said she'll see if she was available.

Cheryl Nickels, hearing Fritz's lawyer, came out of her office. "How can I help you?" asked Cheryl.

"I just came from my client, Fritz, and he says his would-be buyer's lawyer came to visit him and threatened him over losing those guns and ammunition. My client says his life is now in danger and he wants to be moved to protective custody," stated Burt Sterns.

"Who is the would-be buyer? Maybe we can arrest him," stated Cheryl.

"They call him 'Brooks'; he is nobody to mess with, big-time bad news!" declared Sterns. "Messing with Brooks is like committing suicide! Brooks is the only name he goes by."

"I'll check with Milton Bradley and see what he says," replied Cheryl, going back in her office.

"Milton, Fritz's life has just been threatened because he lost the guns and ammunition in the raid and his lawyer wants Fritz to be put under protective custody right away. Fritz might have a visit while in jail."

"Okay, we'll bring Fritz out and put him under protective custody, but we need to arrest the one who threatened him, and arrest the would-be buyer," stated Milton Bradley. "We need Fritz to identify the one who threatened him, and Fritz needs to tell everything he knows about this gun-running and smuggling operation as well."

Milton Bradley called Wayne Milton and told him Fritz's life was in danger, he had been threatened and must be moved right away, but Fritz was to identify the would-be buyer, and the one who threatened him, and he was to tell all he knew about gun-running and smuggling as well.

Wayne understood and agreed after hearing Fritz was threatened.

"Okay, sounds good.." Cheryl told Burt Sterns, who looked relieved.

"Can Fritz be moved right away I'm sure he'll cooperate to spare his life!" stated Burt anxiously.

FBI agents went to the jail, showing their identification, and had the jailer request for Fritz to be released into their custody. Fritz was taken to FBI Director Milton Bradley's office to give a description of the one who threatened him. Milton Bradley was there to question Fritz and get all the information possible about the lawyer and Brooks.

"Oh, I don't know the lawyer; never seen him before, but I figured he must be a lawyer to get in to talk to me, but he said Brooks wants the guns and ammunition, or I may have someone pay me a visit, and he was positive about it."

"Do you know Brooks' name and what he looks like?" asked Milton. "We need a description of the one who threatened you and of Brooks as well. You've got to give us something to work with."

"The lawyer is about 5'9", medium built, dark brown hair, and a fair complexion. Brooks is chunky like a heavy weight wrestler, about 5'10", his head shaved, oily skin, and mean eyes," stated Fritz.

"Okay, do you know where Brooks is located, or how to get hold of him?" asked Wayne.

"I have a phone number I call and leave a message, and then I get a call from an unknown phone number," replied Fritz.

"There are two other things: we only know you as Fritz. What is your real name, your full name? If you cooperate, we protect you! Also, we need you to come clean on your gun-running and smuggling operation." declared Milton Bradley. "Tell us everything you know and did!"

"My name is Fritz Franek," replied Fritz. Fritz told him everything he did, how Brooks contacted him, getting in touch with the gun company given to him by Brooks, and how they were to carry out the gun smuggling. The girls assisted both in the gun smuggling and kidnapping Frieda.

"That is all Marina, Nicole, and Margret did is assist in both the kidnapping and gun-running and smuggling?" asked Milton Bradley.

Fritz replied, "Yes."

"Okay, we'll post bail and claim your civil rights were violated and talk to the judge to get him to go along releasing you, but you will be under constant watch. We'll slip the guns and ammunition into your hands so we can snag this lawyer, Brooks, and the gang together," stated Milton Bradley.

"I understand, but if Brooks smells a rat or senses a trap, he'll be gone, only to return for revenge, and believe me, he knows how!"

"We'll keep that in mind and be very careful," replied Wayne Milton.

"I hope so, or else I'm dead!" declared Fritz.

"Rex, we may need yours and Anne's help, A lawyer for Fritz's would-be buyer for the guns and ammunition has threatened Fritz's life and we have to keep him under protective custody. You and Anne are so good at finding ways to hide people, better than our own agents! We may need your help. This would-be buyer is a very dangerous character and doesn't care that Fritz is in prison. All he cares about is getting his guns and ammunition or else Fritz is dead!" stated Milton Bradley. "Could you and Anne help keep Fritz under wraps until this suspect is caught?"

"What about our safety? If he's as bad as you say, our lives might be in jeopardy," stated Rex. "I knew this break was too good to be real. Anne and I don't trust this Fritz. Can't you move him around and hide him?" asked Rex.

"We can, but we're not up on it like you and Anne; you two are gifted in hiding and evading, more so than our own agents!" stated Milton dryly.

Rex smiled.

"We could use your help in laying a trap for this buyer as well. You would be paid for your service. Oh, by the way, Fritz says Marina, Nicole, and Margret only assisted in the kidnapping, gun-running, and smuggling."

"Let me talk to Anne and see if she's up for it," stated Rex weary.

Rex talked to Anne, she groaned at the thought of hiding, evading, and spying on people so soon, but said if Rex was willing she'd go along.

"I don't want Fritz staying with us though. I don't trust him, and neither do you!" declared Anne.

"I agree, but the way Wayne Milton and Milton Bradley talk, Fritz has broken down and stated the girls only assisted in the kidnapping, gun-running, and smuggling. Fritz is afraid for his life and is cooperating with the District Attorney, FBI, and the Director of Police. According to Wayne and Milton, this buyer is a very dangerous character and Fritz is frantic," stated Rex.

"Oh, they want us to handle this dangerous character, huh?" asked Anne with a smirk.

"They want us to lay a trap for him; all of us would be together on it, and they'll will to pay for our service," replied Rex.

"Oh, I see, we won't be by ourselves, and they're willing to pay for our services. How much?"

"They didn't say, but I imagine it would be a nice amount. We would be doing it more for them than the money," replied Rex with a smile.

"They need to lay out how they aim to keep him under protective custody then," replied Anne dryly.

"I think they're hoping we could help them out on that. I don't think they're too good at it," stated Rex.

"I agree with you there. I could spot their undercover agents every time!" replied Anne with a smirk.

Rex and Anne drove to Wayne Milton's office to go over a setup for a protective custody for Fritz. Rex and Anne stated Fritz staying with them was out of the question.

"What about Heinrich?" stated Anne.

"Oh, Brooks is after Fritz, Heinrich, and the girls are in their cell with no threat to them, just Fritz. I guess Fritz was the only one dealing with Brooks," replied Wayne.

"I suppose he'll need a disguise from time to time?" inquired Anne.

"I suppose, could you help him with that?" asked Wayne.

"As long as Rex stays with me," replied Anne nervously. "I don't trust Fritz!"

"Oh, he is more concerned about staying alive!" replied Wayne. "Believe me on that, he's scared of that Brooks."

"I've heard of him, I believe it," stated Rex. "He is nobody to take lightly from what I've heard!"

"He has been arrested three or four times for first degree murder, three times for felonious assault, and once for blackmail, but never convicted. He has a hot-shot, high-priced lawyer who has kept him out of jail," declared Wayne. "We suspect he's killed more or had it done, but can't prove it. We looked at the lawyer on the video monitor who came to see Fritz. He is a hot-shot lawyer, Frankie Vallenato, and he has represented a lot of bad guys, but keeps himself above the law so we can't touch him. I feel he could tell us a lot if he ever opened up."

"You would have to have something on him, big time, to get him to do that, and good luck on that if he doesn't end up dead first."

replied Rex.

"Yeah, I know," replied Wayne, despaired.

"I could tail him to see if I could get anything on him," stated Anne.

"And tak a chance of gelling killed? No thanks, Anne. These guys play for keeps and they don't even play fair."

Captain Hillary directed the police to surround the warehouse so no one could get away if they try to make an escape. The FBI went in the door the driver, two body guards, and Brooks went in. They were all in a room looking the rifles over and checking them out, plus two big crates were full of ammunition.

"Okay, fellows, we're the FBI! Put your hands up high and no funny business!" declared Milton Bradley with his .357 drawn, and the other FBI agents' guns drawn as well.

The suspects noticing they are surrounded and outnumbered, put their hands up, but Brooks made a run, but realized that would be a mistake, too many guns pointing at them. After the suspects were handcuffed, Bradley and the FBI firearms expert walked over to look at the rifles and ammunition; all accounted for.

"Exactly what were you going to do with these? Start a war? Or were you going to ship them to Columbia?" demanded Milton Bradley.

No reply.

"Okay, don't talk, but you will talk sooner or later! Mark my word on that!" snarled Bradley.

"That depends on what our lawyers have to say," growled Brooks.

"Well, hello, Brooks! So nice to see you again!" laughed Milton Bradley.

"Up yours too!" replied Brooks, glaring at Bradley.

"Oh, be nice now, being nasty isn't going to help you at all! You are going to be in interrogation!" replied Bradley laughing hideously.

The news reporters, ABC News, and NBC Live mainly, arrived to catch the suspects' arrests.

All the suspects handcuffed were led to waiting squad cars as the news reporters' record them for the evening news, to be taken to lock-up and questioned separately to see who would start talking first. Brooks was locked in a separate cell so he couldn't silence the others and let him sweat.

Being that the warehouse was a crime scene, it was taped off and a lock placed on all the doors. Captain Hillary and Milton Bradley went back to the warehouse to do a search from top to bottom for anything that could be used in court. An address book and phone number to somewhere in Columbia was found in a bottom desk drawer along with a map of an area encircled. On the wall was a calendar with a scenery picture of a beautiful flower garden. Checking the different months, certain days were circled; maybe one of the suspects would disclose what the circled days meant.

Fritz was moved to an undisclosed safehouse. What would happen to him was undecided; the D.A. would go easier on him now. Heinrich and the girls, their role was yet to be determined. A watch was kept on the girls. They were depressed at what might become of them, never being locked up before.

Rex and Anne, watching the news, heard the would-he buyers of the guns and ammunition had been arrested and the rifles and ammunition seized. Captain Hillary directed the police surrounding the warehouse to prevent an escape.

"Oh, alright, Captain Hillary!" exclaimed Rex and Anne, laughing.

"Captain Hillary is back in action!" declared Rex, calling the captain to let him know that he and Anne heard about him in the warehouse raid on the news.

"Yeah, I was there, directing the officers to surround the warehouse so none of the suspects could escape. It was all over in a few minutes," replied the Captain.

"So, you're back in action. Good for you!" declared Anne on the other phone.

"It feels good to be back in action too," declared Captain Hillary happily. "There were no news reporters there until after the raid because we wanted to surprise the suspects and we didn't know if we could with news reporters there."

"What about Fritz? I suppose he's tucked away someplace safe?" asked Rex.

"Oh yeah. I don't know where, but they took him somewhere, I suppose a safehouse. Heinrich and the girls' roles have yet to be determined," stated Hillary.

"I figure Fritz was the main culprit, and yet he is the one who bellied up to save his skin!" stated Rex.

"If he hadn't talked, he would've been killed for not getting those rifles and ammunition to Brooks, who doesn't accept excuses."

"Now they'll investigate him and he'll go up big time for all he has done! He probably realizes it too," stated Anne.

"Oh, yeah, he will if his lawyers don't find a legal technical loophole or something to bail him out," replied Hillary. "His past-ins with the law will be considered as well."

"There is always that legal technicality, isn't there?" growled Rex.

"It is to protect the 'supposedly' innocent until they are proven guilty."

"So, how does it feel to be Chief of Police again?" asked Rex.

"Oh, it feels great. Now I can go on with my career and fulfill my destiny; this is my home away from home!" exclaimed Captain Hillary happily.

"Good, both Anne and I are happy for you!"

Brooks realized he was in a bad fix unless his lawyers could find a legal technicality to bail him out. The FBI would keep on investigating and questioning the crew until they broke down and got them to talk, and they would be interrogating him as well. "That Bradley said I will be 'special' in interrogating me! I will do big time, this time, unless I can make a deal! Darn!"

"Well, I'm glad this is over and done with," Rex told Anne.

"Me too, now if I can avoid the sniper!" replied Anne. "I wonder how Karl, Gertrud, and Frieda are doing. Have you heard from them lately?"

"No, but I figure they're trying to get to a life of peace and quiet away from the public eye and the press," stated Rex.

Fritz overheard there had been a reward posted by word-of-mouth from Brooks to take care of Fritz permanently. "I've got to get out of here and disappear." He started looking for opportunities to escape and totally disappear. "Heinrich and the girls can make it on their own; I'm sure they'll be okay."

Fritz, watching the laundry attendants loading and unloading clean laundry from a unique laundry van hit on a plan. On delivery day, Fritz waited until the dirty uniforms and laundry were mostly loaded into the van, and quickly ducked into the van, moving to the front behind barrels of dirty laundry as the guy went for another barrel. The loaded van drove away as Fritz changed into a slightly dirty uniform and moved part way toward the door and waited for the door to be opened. The laundry guy opened the door to load more dirty uniforms and laundry into the van. While the guy went for another barrel, Fritz quickly hopped out and slipped away into a gym three blocks away to change into street clothes. He disappeared into the crowd going about their business.

The security at the safehouse, discovering Fritz missing, looked for him, but he gone! The police and FBI were notified and there was an all-out bulletin put out for Fritz to be brought back. This time, he would be put in a maximum-security prison! An inquiry revealed Fritz must have escaped on the laundry van, but where was he now?

Hillary called Rex to tell him Fritz was on the loose and hadn't been located yet. Alarmed, Rex told Anne.

"You think he'll come after us?" Anne asked Rex.

"Hard to say. We did cause his arrest, but he might just make a run to disappear," replied Rex. "He could be anywhere by now."

Fritz's picture was on the news that he had escaped; *Good luck finding him*, Rex felt. Anne decided to stay with Rex until Fritz is caught. A bulletin was posted on the news, post office, banks, and in the newspaper with Fritz Franek's picture and description.

An escaped suspect in an illegal arms smuggling conspiracy. If you see him, do not approach, but contact the police or FBI.

Brooks, hearing Fritz had escaped, contacted one of his goons through his lawyer to find Fritz and take care of him. Brooks thought of a way to get out himself, but security around him was pretty tight. If he could trade places with one of the transferees temporarily, he might be able to escape unnoticed. Brooks started thinking and planning.

There was one prisoner, Melvin Snyder, about the same height and weight as Brooks; to be transfer to a minimum-security prison soon. Brooks studied Snyder's habits and movements. On the day Snyder was to be transferred, Brooks mingled with him in the prison yard as Snyder went to the restroom. Brooks followed him to waylay him switching uniform with Snyder's name tag. Brooks mistaken for Snyder, boarded the prison bus to the minimum-security prison. Stopping for gas and to stretch, Brooks claimed he needed to use the restroom. He went, but ducked out the exit door to a garage, clobbered a customer, changed clothes in the storage room, and then slipped away, mistaken as a civilian disappearing. Now Brooks had escaped and was on the run, as well as Fritz! Brooks' picture and description was posted on the news.

Captain Hillary, alarmed, called Rex to warn him, and Rex told Hillary, "Anne and I saw it on the news. We're on the lookout for both; either one might figure they have a score to settle, or they might just want to disappear. Anne is staying with me until they are caught."

As time went by and both Fritz and Brooks weren't caught, they could be anywhere! The airports, train, and transit stations were put on alert, as well the seaports. A railroad worker in Fresno reported seeing someone jumping aboard a moving boxcar, but after searching the train an hour later, the suspicious person wasn't to be found. The description fit Fritz, but if it was him, he kept moving on. Brooks had gone underground. Time went on and there was no news of either one; they both had disappeared. They both were put on the 'Wanted' list by the FBI. Interpol was notified. Rex and Anne hopefully felt they'd never see either one of them ever again.

Rex and Anne visited each other every day, sometimes grilling on Rex's deck, and other times on Anne's deck. Sgt. Judy Sturgis and Kory Bishop continued to grow closer and more serious about each other; it looked like weeding bells were in the near future. Everything was turning out perfect, but Rex continued to feel there was another big case waiting around the corner, but would enjoy the moment of peace and quiet for now. What happened, would happen; so be it. Rex's feeling was right, there was another big case waiting for him, and it would take both he and Anne to solve it! *So be it, just enjoy the moment for now.*

Captain Hillary now lived in his new house in a much nicer neighborhood, enjoyed his backyard, and grilled every once in a while. Jan Roberts and Harold Jacobs continued reporting the news, local news, that was, until Rex and Anne once again hit the news. Anne sensed there would be another big case soon, but also wanted to enjoy the current calm.

Rex and Anne visited both his parents and her mother and sister, sensing something was about to throw them into another big case, just a matter of time. Captain Hillary felt it would be soon as well, a most uncomfortable feeling, and stayed in communication with Rex and Anne.

Just a matter of time before another big case, but Rex and Anne enjoyed what time they had of peace and quiet.

Anna Towers

When Anna Towers was a little girl, she watched secretaries working in offices and decided she wanted to work in an office. She became the high school classroom secretary, and then part-time secretary for the school administration. Going on to college, she took up bookkeeping and accounting paid by her inheritance, being she was an "A" student in Math in school.

Looking for work as a bookkeeper/account wasn't exactly plentiful, so she took a job as a secretary at Scott Pitters & Associates Law Firm, but looking for a job as a bookkeeper/account. As she was about to give up looking, the Militia's Militia sent her a letter inviting her to come for an interview for bookkeeping and accounting. Anna was thrilled.

Going to apply for the job, she got the job that day, She went out to dinner with a few friends from her old job as secretary. The managing staff noticed Anna was good with figures, and word was passed on to upper management.

Suzy Goutily came over to Anna one day to comment her on management taking notice of her. "You're fixing to move up the ladder to your own office, I hear. Congratulations!"

"What are you talking about?" asked Anna surprised.

"Oh, you don't know?" asked Suzy laughing. "Stop being modest, you've been bumping for position and now you're fixing to get it!"

"I don't know what you're talking about, Suzy, please explain," stated Anna Towers.

"You don't know? Management is thinking of giving you your own office as bookkeeper/accountant, but remember, with that position comes more responsibilities as well as higher pay." declared Suzy.

"Are you serious? I'm fixing to get my own office?" asked Anna, stunned.

"That's what I overheard in the inter office," exclaimed Suzy.

"I guess being good at math and going to college for bookkeeping and accounting paid off," exclaimed Anna happily.

"Yeah, but a lot will be required of you too. I suspect you'll earn your pay!" declared Suzy.

"Well, nothing comes free if it's worth having," replied Anna.

"I wish you the best, just don't forget about us lowly secretaries," replied Suzy.

"Hey, if I do get that job, my door will be open to you all whenever you choose to visit," declared Anna. "Getting that job won't turn my nose up at you all."

"I hope not, we all like you, one or two might get a bit jealous though."

"I will still be Anna Towers who got a break!"

Sure enough, that late afternoon Anna was called to the office of Mr. Frank Broccoli; Mr. Leonard Toffees, Gertrud Strafford, and Sully Brantford were there as well.

"Hi, Anna, how would you like to have your own office as bookkeeper/accountant?" "My own office, sir?" asked Anna surprised, but happy.

"Yes, you were an 'A' student in Math in school and you went on to college for bookkeeping and accounting and did really well! We feel you could be an immense help in our accounting."

"Thank you, I appreciate your thinking of me so highly! I hardly know what to say other than to say. Thank you!"

"Oh, you'll earn your pay if you accept the job," stated Mr. Toffees Mr. Broccoli and Gertrud Strafford nodded in agreement.

"Where will my office be, if I may inquire?" asked Anna.

"Across from the secretaries' work area," declared Gertrud Strafford. "Your salary will be $500.00 a week, four weeks' vacation time, and your own health insurance coverage."

"That sounds good, I like that," declared Anna happily.

"Then you accept?" asked Broccoli.

"Yes!" exclaimed Anna Towers happily.

With that, they shook hands and congratulated her.

Anna, returning to her desk beaming, looked at the empty office across from the secretaries' work area. Suzy, smiling at Anna beaming, said out loud, "Anna took the job as bookkeeper/accountant! She'll have her own office now!"

The secretaries all looked at Anna curious and smiling.

"Are you going to still know us?" asked Sharon Tomsky.

"Yes, of course! My office will be open to you any time you want to visit!" declared Anna.

With that, Anna gathered her personal things and took them to the office, arranging things to her taste. The chair, an executive chair, Anna sat to see how it felt to sit behind a big desk with an executive phone with a row of buttons to different departments and a message recorder.

Mr. Broccoli came to Anna's new office to let her know her phone will be ready for to use in a couple of hours. "How do you like your chair, comfortable?"

"Yes, very comfortable," replied Anna, smiling.

"Tomorrow morning will be your official first day in this office as bookkeeper/accountant," stated Mr. Broccoli.

Gertrud brought a desk pad, a pen holder set with pens and pencils, whiteout, a desk calendar, and a desk clock all black and gold.

"It's going to take a while to grasp this is really my office," stated Anna.

"Well, we're glad you like it," replied Gertrud. "If there's anything you need or any questions, just press the red button."

As time went on, Anna became accustomed to Militia's Militia's procedure, their bookkeeping and accounting procedures, doing transactions and transfers, faxing and receiving documents, etc. The day-to-day business of the militia became a daily routine job for Anna. She became friends with the three secretaries, Alia Stevenson, Betsy Owens, Tricia Bussone, and the staff she worked with; it was like family working there. After a year, Anna took notice that some of the transactions, transfers, and documents were questionable, and there were large money transfers to banks out of the country to countries with no treaties with the U.S. Anna felt it would be unsafe, much less unwise, to question the staff about this.

As time went on, Anna decided if the money transfers disappeared, the militia wouldn't be able to file charges because of illegal practices, but they would take care of the matter in other ways. Anna heard that one man, Arthur Ward, a maintenance man, was caught stealing from the firm, and now he hadn't been seen since. Maybe he skipped to another state, but no, Anna heard he was dominated.

These guys are sore losers! Anna dismissed the thought of stealing from this company. The new maintenance man was Carl Pismo, sort of quiet type, who did his job well.

As time went on, the staff became confident and depended on Anna more every day. Anna was like one of the group and met some of the more important staff members. But Anna worked in her office which was clear across the hall from the staff offices, and you needed a good reason be over there! The secretaries never had any reason to be over there, but stayed in their own work area, and even had a separate entrance/exit. That was, more or less, expressed to Anna by a secretary, Alai Stevenson. To be over there without a reason was a big no-no.

"Why is it such a bad idea to go over there?" asked Anna.

"Oh, the celebrities and big shots have conferences with the staff, and to overhear or see anything we're not supposed to is a big no-no," explained Alai. "Whatever they discuss that is so secretive, I don't know, but it's not smart to be over there!"

Hearing this, Anna became alarmed wondering what kind of company or firm she worked for. Anna looked every time a celebrity or big shot came in, making a mental note of their faces. Anna felt being caught with a camera would be just as bad as being over there, so she memorized their faces. Anna felt she couldn't keep working here for long; they were involved in something illegal, and she was their bookkeeper/accountant!

Anna thought about applying for another job and expressed that to Alia, but she backed away.

"Ah, I don't know, but I'd say they would feel you know too much of the business now, being their bookkeeper/accountant," said Alai quietly. "What us three secretaries handle is just simple, ordinal office stuff, but what you do is totally different!"

"Yeah, I guess it is…" replied Anna thoughtfully.

From that day, Anna figured out a way to disappear, start over. *I have my inheritance from my father, but I don't want to spend all of that in hiding and running!* Then Anna thought of a way to scheme money from this firm to run, hide, and start over. *I'll for sure enough need to hide then!*

Anna memorized what she knew about the firm so she would have something to bargain with if she was ever arrested. *How did I get into this mess?* Anna wondered. *Now I must get myself out of it!*

Anna checked on her home computer the different overseas banks and what their procedure was for opening an account. The Swiss bank Anna heard was a favorite with a lot of firms and businesses wanting to hide their money. Anna checked the militia's transfers, drafts, and statements as they came across her desk for business with any Swiss banks. There was one with two different Swiss banks, the Swiss National Bank and The Bank of Swaziland one bank in Columbia.

There were no transfer transactions, drafts, or statements from the Bahamas banks. Anna, on her home computer, faxed an inquiry to the Bahama State Bank about their procedure in starting a new account and deposits of large sums of money. She received a brochure about their business practices and procedures, including large deposits. Anna opened an account with the Bahama State Bank; it was ready for Anna to send any drafts or large deposits.

Now the next giant step, if she didn't get caught: How do you withdraw large sums of cash without someone taking notice?

Anna discovered if she transferred the money before it went to deposit, then she could withdraw or transfer the money to wherever she desired. Anna, working at her desk, was handed a transfer deposit slip for one hundred million dollars to go the Swiss National Bank for deposit. Anna was to process the transfer to the Swiss National Bank from the Oakland State bank, People's State Bank, and the

Anna waited until almost closing time for the Bahama State Bank before transferring the large deposits from the three banks in an interest savings acme. It was just about quitting time at the Militia's Militia Building as well, and the three secretaries had already left for the day. Anna decided it was time for her to leave as well.

On the way home, Anna stopped at Warehouse Storage & Moving Supply store to buy a lot of storage and shipping boxes, then headed home. Arriving home at her apartment, Anna had a bite to eat and then packed everything in boxes. After clothes and shoes and personal things were packed and sealed in boxes, she loaded everything she could into her van until it was full. Anna drove a ways in the country to smash her computer in case the militia could trace that computer.

Leaving the furniture, she left for the expressway to head where she would lease likely be found, driving all night and part of the next day, only stopping for gas, got a bite to eat, and used the restroom, then got back on the expressway.

"I'm going to need a whole new identity change, name and address, date of my birth, and social security number!" Anna tells herself. "Who do I know that can and will do that?"

Thinking hard, there was a man she stumbled across once who had done that on a rare occasion. Locating him, she asked him to help her. She gave a sad story of how she had gone to work for a firm and discovered they were into illegal firearms and contraband and shipping them to rebel forces in Columbia. "Sammy", feeling sorry for Anna, agreed to make the false identity papers for her, which took a day to make. Anna gave him $500.00 and left to travel the rest of the day and all night. The next day she stopped at a small off-the-road motel and café to eat and sleep through to the next morning, then driving another day.

Stopping off in Las Vegas, Anna looked for a computer store and found one. She bought a new Windows 8 laptop. Going back to her car, Anna looked up a likely place to hide out until she decided to settle down. Anna found an apartment to rent for now.

Contacting the Bahama State Bank, she put in a transfer request to transfer the interest, wigs avoid to the Nevada state Bank. There she could withdraw the money as she needed it for now before moving again. Anna realized that to stay ahead of the militia she would have to stay on the move for a very long time.